CW00349369

Dead Spit

When government vet Linus Rintoul bumps into an old friend of his mother's, she is unusually relieved at being recognized and he learns that she has recently returned to Britain after many years abroad, only to find someone else with her name, her address and her reputation as a breeder of Antiguan Truffle Dogs.

Linus's attempts to help her get to the bottom of the mystery take him into the esoteric world of pedigree dogs, where it is soon made abundantly clear to him that his incursion is resented. The impostor is determined not to be exposed. But with murder and terrorism becoming unexpected accompaniments to an otherwise harmless activity, Linus can no longer stand aside, and the prestigious Crufts Dog Show proves to be far more exciting than he had bargained for . . .

by the same author

DOG'S BODY

JANET EDMONDS

Dead Spit

To Carol —

hoping your dog-show days are a bit less fraught than this!

Janet Edmonds.

COLLINS, 8 GRAFTON STREET, LONDON W1

William Collins Sons & Co. Ltd
London · Glasgow · Sydney · Auckland
Toronto · Johannesburg

First published 1989

British Library Cataloguing in Publication Data

Edmonds, Janet
Dead spit.—(Crime Club)
I. Title
823'.914[F]

ISBN 0 00 232246 3

Photoset in Linotron Baskerville by
Rowland Phototypesetting Ltd
Bury St Edmunds, Suffolk
Printed in Great Britain by
William Collins Sons & Co. Ltd, Glasgow

AUTHOR'S NOTE

The security procedures described in this story are deliberately not the ones which would be employed in the circumstances described.

CHAPTER 1

Edith Ledwell looked at the long queue of barely moving cars on the other side of the road.

'It looks as if we're nearly there,' she said.

'We are,' the cabbie told her. 'Just down that road. D'you want to walk? It's only a few hundred yards and it'll be a lot quicker.'

'Less frustrating, too, I imagine. Yes, I think I will. How much do I owe you?'

She paid him and thanked him and then waited for a brief gap in the traffic before crossing briskly over, threading her way between the bumpers of the line of estate cars and making considerably better time than they towards the entrance to Perry Park. It had been something of a disappointment to learn that the dog show was no longer part of a much larger City show because she had always enjoyed seeing the horticultural section, the rabbits and the handicrafts. Still, it was the dogs she'd come to see and they had always been the largest section, so perhaps it was hardly surprising they had finally taken over the whole shebang.

She made her way across the car park and noted that the City fathers had still not seen fit to drain the land adequately here. There had been rain in the past week, not all that much but enough to leave the lower-lying part of the huge site spongy and black where yesterday's cars and dogs had churned it up. Bearded Collies and Bobtails were being carried into the showground, draped round their owners' necks like Biblical sheep. Others were sporting little raincoats: four rain-proofed trouser-legs attached to a body that zipped up along the spine, the long fur of their dangling ears encased in plastic bags. To the observer they looked ridiculous. In breeds where presentation could decide who won, the sniggers of the uninformed were a tiny price to pay for the occasional red card or the even more elusive green-and-white one that would ultimately contribute to the dog's acquiring the title 'Champion'.

As she went through the gate into the showground itself, Edith Ledwell began to feel quite excited. It was a long, long time since she had been to a dog show. It must be all of twenty years, and more than that since she had been to one in England. When she and Ralph had emigrated to Australia she had been to one or two, but without any dogs to show it had seemed too much of an anti-climax to induce her to repeat the experience very often, and besides, Ralph's health—the reason they had emigrated in the first place—had not initially left her much time for dog shows, and none at all for dogs. They'd never regretted emigrating. It had been a long, slow haul before Ralph's health had benefited from it, but it finally did and he had lived until last year. When they had left England, no one would have given much for Ralph's chances of making fifty, much less nearly eighty! Now, his estate settled, she was back, as much for old times' sake as anything else. She had no idea whether she would decide to settle here again. It had certainly been a possibility at the back of her mind when she had set out. She'd taken a short-term let on a rather nice little ground-floor flat in North Oxford, their old stomping ground, but their old acquaintance in this country seemed to have died or moved away and this nostalgic visit was proving to be rather a depressing one. It was beginning to look as if she'd be happier going back to Australia where they had a circle of friends.

She certainly had no intention of going back into dogs. She was seventy-two and had no desire to become embroiled once more in the highly competitive and therefore frequently unpleasant world of pedigree dogs. If she were content to stay on the sidelines, showing one or two middling-to-good animals, collecting seconds and thirds and the occasional first, she'd pose no threat to anyone and would probably enjoy the days out, but she knew herself better than to delude herself that she would be content with that. In the old days, she had had the best. Within her breed, she had been quite a big fish. Of course, it had been a very small pond, but all the same she had had good dogs and had been known to have them and consequently they had won—sometimes, it had to be admitted, when they hadn't deserved to. If she went back into dogs—it would have to be a small breed this time—she would want to rebuild her reputation to that level. No, at seventy-two it would be much wiser to stay out of the contest altogether. When she had decided what she was going to do, whether to stay in England or return to Australia, she'd get herself a little waif and stray from the dogs' home—an old one, like herself, not some boisterous puppy—and that would be companionship for her. She'd get a mongrel because that way its faults wouldn't niggle at her every time she looked at it. In the meantime it was going to be quite interesting to see what sort of progress the breed she had introduced and campaigned for all those years ago had made in the last quarter of a century.

The old priorities began to assert themselves. First, get a catalogue before they sell out. Then locate the lavatories and, if by some fluke there wasn't a queue yet, use them. Finally, since she didn't have a dog, find the refreshment tent and have some coffee. That would give her the chance to study the catalogue. There wasn't much point in going round the benches until most of the dogs were there and their owners had begun to relax a bit after the journey.

She turned to the index page. Alaskan Malamutes, Anatolian Karabash. Yes, here they were—Antiguan Truffle Dogs. Good heavens! As many as that! A hundred and five dogs making a hundred and thirty-two entries. It was incredible. She cast her eye down the page. Not the biggest entry but certainly up there in—what?—the top ten. And to think they used to regard twenty dogs as a good entry! It was a recollection that made her feel very old and very out-of-touch. Maybe she shouldn't have come. She sipped her coffee and then sat gazing in the direction of the doorway, absent-mindedly turning her wedding-ring round on her finger. Perhaps she should make her way back to Birmingham New Street and catch the next train back to Oxford. Or turn this visit into a shopping-trip—have lunch in Rackham's and 'do' the Bull Ring. She shook herself. This was being too silly for words. Now that she was here she'd have a look at her old breed and if she liked what she saw on the benches she'd watch the judging. She wouldn't say who she was—the chances were none of the present-day ATD fanciers would have known her anyway, though she supposed they might have heard of her and if she did say who she was there would either be patent disbelief or squeals of excitement and she'd be introduced to everyone. It was difficult to decide which prospect horrified her the most.

She turned to the order of judging. Ring 17—Antiguan Truffle Dogs—first in the ring. She glanced at her watch. Half past ten and judging began at ten. They must be well into the first Puppy class by now, possibly further. She stood up and drained the last of her coffee before making her way across to the ring.

It was one of those shows where you were expected to bring your own chair and Edith hadn't, but someone kindly offered her husband's seat.

'He's gone to the beer tent,' she said. 'He won't be back this side of one o'clock. He's not really interested in the dogs, so you might as well have it for the time being.'

Edith thanked her and sank gratefully down into it. She glanced at the ring. The breed seemed bigger than it used to be and although these animals didn't quite look adult, they seemed, with one or two exceptions, too mature to be puppies. Juniors, perhaps.

'Which class?' she asked her neighbour.

'Puppy Dog. You've missed Minor Puppy—there were only two in it.'

Edith watched the dogs for a while without bothering to refer to the catalogue. The names wouldn't mean much to her anyway, not after all this time. Probably the pedigrees wouldn't, either. Presentation was better than it used to be —much better. The tight, sandy curls gleamed in the autumn sunlight—no mean achievement in that colour and texture, and the characteristic smooth strip down the spine shone like satin on most dogs, though there were one or two where she had a strong suspicion that clever use of a stripping comb had been necessary to achieve that three-inch smooth strip. Movement was good, she noticed with approval and some surprise. Movement tended to be the first thing to suffer when a breed became popular. Perhaps the upsurge in numbers was relatively recent and built on a very sound base. It can't have been easy to achieve this sort of popularity when one considered the breed's peculiar breeding pattern.

'Do they still have small litters?' she asked.

'Not as small as they used to be. That was before we came into them, of course. I believe breeders used to count themselves lucky if they had two in a litter. Now we expect four. My vet says it's due to improved feeding. They breed every year now, too. Same reason, I suppose.'

Edith supposed so, too, and felt a little sad. There had been a real sense of achievement every time a bitch produced its singleton in alternate years. It had made it a breed for the devotee.

Puppy Dog was judged and the prize-cards and rosettes handed out and Junior Dog came into the ring. It was a big class and a good one. Size had definitely changed, Edith decided, and in an indefinable way so had type but the overall impression was of quality. Movement was good in this class, too.

'They all seem to move very well,' she remarked.

'They do, don't they? We can thank Mrs Ledwell for that. She's very hot on movement.'

Edith was startled. She must have misheard. Of course, she always had been very hot on movement, but surely her companion had used the present tense?

'Mrs Ledwell?' she queried.

Her companion nodded in the direction of the ring. 'The little old lady over there—second from the left. She'll probably win this class: that's a super youngster she's showing. She's done a lot with it. She introduced the breed, you know, and now she keeps us all on the straight and narrow. Sweet woman.'

It was an unusual commendation to hear at a ringside, Edith thought. Perhaps the dog scene had changed more than she realized. She looked across at the little old lady. She was roughly the same age and build as Edith with similarly grey hair but Edith thought the other woman might be rather more frail. She certainly didn't waste much money on clothes. She was dressed neatly enough but the colours were muddy and the garments, though clean, were shapeless. They did nothing to set off the colour of her dogs. Edith had always prided herself on dressing well and in a manner that complemented the sandy coats. These thoughts went through her mind with an insistence that far exceeded their importance, as if Edith were evading the more puzzling information she had just been given.

She opened her catalogue, turned to the ATD section and ran her finger down the alphabetical list of exhibitors. Here it was. Ledwell, Mrs E. So what? she told herself. Lots of people had the same name as someone else. Look at all the John Smiths in the world. But her eye had gone on beyond the name to the address and the comforting thought had lost its power to comfort almost before it had been conceived. Fireaway Cottage, Lower Shottington. Her stomach turned over in a fear that was almost superstitious. This was impossible. It simply couldn't happen. Coincidences occurred but never on this scale. She cast her eye on down the page. The other Mrs Ledwell had entered no fewer than six dogs, all home-bred. It came as no surprise to observe that they all carried Edith's old affix. She'd compounded it for life in the old days when that was possible, so it wasn't a case of someone applying to use a lapsed kennel name.

A wave of panic swept over her, the unpleasant feeling that she didn't exist, that she was a figment of her own imagination and that this other Edith Ledwell, with the right kind of dogs, the right address and the right affix, was the real one. She told herself firmly that this was nonsense, that there was some very simple explanation. The trouble was, she hadn't the slightest idea what it might be.

Politely enthusiastic clapping greeted Mrs Ledwell's win and Edith's companion glanced at her.

'Are you all right?' she asked. 'You look quite pale.'

Edith summoned up what she hoped was a convincing smile. 'Thank you, yes. It's probably just the sun. At my age, you know . . .' She let her voice tail off as if her age explained everything. It needed to, she thought. The sun wasn't that hot. Her instinct was to get up and run, to put as much distance between herself and this other Mrs Ledwell as she could in the hope that by so doing she could somehow put things back as they had been before she came here. That hope was impossible of achievement, of course, so she forced herself to stay where she was until the next class was well under way and then she thanked her companion for the loan of the chair, murmured something about having just caught sight of someone she hadn't seen for ages and beat a retreat without too much apparent haste. She headed for the beer tent, bought herself a gin-and-tonic and sat down to think.

It was a singularly unproductive exercise. She could, she supposed, go to the Kennel Club stand and say, 'That woman's pretending to be me,' but their reaction was all too foreseeable. They would smile politely, probably take down details and as likely as not, put them in the bin as soon as she walked away. Or they would ask—very nicely, no doubt—why someone should be doing such a thing, and the truth was, Edith couldn't think of any plausible explanation. In fact, it was much more likely that the consensus would be that it was she, Edith, who was trying to claim another woman's identity. The fact that the other Mrs Ledwell had obviously been around for some years and was well known lent credence to her, not to Edith. Nor was there much point in going to the police. Even if they believed her and she were ultimately proved right, what crime had been committed? It was almost certainly no crime to assume a name, or to live in a house that the original owner of that name had previously lived in unless it was done as a means of defrauding people, and it was hard to see how the other one was doing that. She might be trading on Edith's name and reputation but she must have been doing so for some time and there was nothing second-rate about her dogs, no matter what name she exhibited them under. What's more, she was unlikely to be making much out of them, no matter how successful they were. Perhaps the answer was to tackle her directly.

This was not an appealing idea but she rather thought she had little choice but to carry it through. After all, if she did decide to lodge a complaint with someone, the first question they would ask was likely to be, 'And what explanation does she give?'

She waited until the judging was over and then went to the marquee where the breed was benched. There was a bustle of people congratulating Mrs Ledwell on having won both Challenge Certificates. It was, Edith gathered, the bitch's first and the dog's third and qualifying one. From today, subject to Kennel Club confirmation, he added the magical word 'Champion' to his name. Mrs Ledwell accepted the congratulations with a self-deprecating humility that probably explained the description 'sweet woman'. It struck Edith as phoney but then she was hardly an impartial observer. She let the other exhibitors return to their benches and their coffee-flasks before adding her own congratulations to the others.

Mrs Ledwell thanked her politely but with no particular interest. Edith was just another complete stranger. Of one thing Edith was quite sure. If Mrs Ledwell had ever seen her in the days before she emigrated, she didn't recognize her.

'I understand you're the person who introduced this breed,' she said.

Mrs Ledwell looked a little surprised that there was to be a conversation, but she smiled with her accustomed modesty. 'That's right. More years ago than I care to admit to,' and she laughed conspiratorially, as if Edith, being of the same generation, would know just how she felt.

'And you've had them all that time!' Edith injected just the right amount of amazed admiration into her voice and was rewarded with a decidedly sharpened interest.

Mrs Ledwell's eyes narrowed almost imperceptibly. 'No, I haven't, as a matter of fact. I got the breed established and then we had to emigrate because of my husband's health: there was something about it in the dog press at the time, actually. When he died I came back and took them up again.' There was a finality in her tone which Edith decided to ignore.

'Your old friends must have been pleased to see you back,' she commented.

There was an infinitesimal pause before Mrs Ledwell answered. 'You'd think so, wouldn't you? I was quite looking forward to seeing . . . all my old friends but it was over fifteen years and would you believe not one of the people involved in Truffle Dogs when I came back had been associated with them before? There had been a complete change.'

'You mean they were all newcomers?'

'Far from it. They'd just come into the breed after I left and the handful of people I'd known had simply dropped out. It wasn't a commercial breed, of course, and they do say most people who come into dogs only last five years.'

'So I've heard,' Edith agreed truthfully, 'and if they last ten, you can regard them as permanent. They must have regarded you as a legend come to life.'

'I think they did, rather. Of course, there were one or two people in other breeds who knew me before but fifteen years is a long time and even they said they probably wouldn't have recognized me if the name hadn't tipped them off. Once it had, they said they thought I'd worn rather well, which was nice of them.'

'It was, wasn't it?' Edith said, forming her own opinion of their powers of observation. 'I was sitting next to someone at the ringside who was telling me you even came back to the same house. That must have been a stroke of luck.'

Mrs Ledwell frowned. 'It wasn't quite as lucky as it sounded. I was living somewhere else for quite a while and then my old cottage came on the market and I managed to snap it up. That's when I decided to go back into the breed, as a matter of fact: it seemed like Kismet.' She gave a laugh that in a younger—a much younger—woman might have been described as coy and turned back to her dogs. 'Were you thinking of having a Truffler?' she asked.

Edith hesitated. 'I did have some such idea when I came here, but really I think I'd be better off with something smaller. Not that they're a large breed, but I'm not getting any younger and we have to look ahead, don't we? After all, any dog I buy is likely still to be with me in ten or twelve years' time and by then I don't suppose I could still cope.'

Mrs Ledwell looked her up and down in a way that was, Edith felt, unnecessarily dispassionate. 'You're probably right. I'm fortunate in having my son to help me out. Dogs can be such a tie, though. One has to think it through very carefully before committing oneself, I always say.'

Edith found nothing to disagree with in that, although she wasn't too happy to be given to understand that she looked like someone who would not be able to cope with what she knew to be a very easy breed. She took her leave and drifted off, as people did at dog shows. She understood how Mrs Ledwell had earned the epithet, 'a sweet woman', but she had a shrewd suspicion that the marshmallow coating covered a very hard kernel.

She made her way across to the Kennel Club stand where three bandbox-neat young women in Kennel Club green answered queries from the straightforward to the bizarre with unruffled courtesy.

'I wonder if you can help me,' she began diffidently and was accorded an encouraging smile. 'If the use of a compounded affix lapses and is then taken up again after an interval of some years, does the Kennel Club check that the "new" user is the same as the old one?'

This was obviously one of the more bizarre questions, but the girl's confident smile faltered only briefly. 'Oh, I'm sure we do. It would be rather important, wouldn't it?'

'How?'

The girl was taken aback. 'I beg your pardon? I don't quite follow.'

'How do you check? I mean, do you hire a private detective, or what?'

'Well, I don't know—I mean, there are signatures and things, aren't there?'

A man who had been hovering in the background moved forward. 'I couldn't help overhearing your query, madam. Have you reason to believe someone is using an affix to which they're not entitled?'

Edith hesitated. All she had intended was a simple answer to a simple question. She wasn't at all sure what she wanted to do about it at this stage or, indeed, *whether* she wanted to do anything about it.

'No, not at all,' she said hastily. 'I was just curious. It was just an idle question.' She turned away.

The man and the girl exchanged glances and shrugged. 'Do we?' the girl asked.

'How can we? We compare signatures, but signatures change over the years anyway. If it's the same name and the same address, we take it on trust. Wouldn't you?'

CHAPTER 2

Linus Rintoul hesitated on the steps of the Ashmolean and stared at the rain teeming down. Great, slanting sheets of it cunningly angled so that, no matter which direction you took, it was always in your face. And always on his day off. He didn't always have the same day off: he had no ties, no wife to grumble if her plans were overset, so if the office schedules had to be rearranged, he was the first choice for a change of day. He was quite happy with this: it didn't happen all that often and, when it did, it stopped monotony moving in. Yet the Almighty knew with unerring accuracy when he would be free, and then it rained. He grinned to himself and a woman coming up the steps towards him gave him a slightly wider berth. Men in raincoats who grinned as you came towards them were best avoided. He supposed a theologian would say it proved the omnipotence of the Almighty. Linus was inclined to think it proved his bloody-mindedness but that was probably blasphemy. Whatever the reason, he was strongly of the opinion that, if only he could be bothered to keep a record of each day's weather, it would prove to be glorious on every day that he wasn't free. He snorted. The exhibition had been a little disappointing, too. He owed himself a treat.

He turned his collar up and ran down the steps, across the road against the traffic—it was too wet to bother with that confounded Pelican crossing—and into the Randolph. Tea was what he wanted. Not some overbrewed cup you could hide a mouse in but Earl Grey, with neat little triangular sandwiches and scones with butter and strawberry jam and cream. Enough cholesterol to send you to your grave content.

He hung up his raincoat and cap and automatically straightened his jacket and fingered his tie. The Randolph always had that sort of effect. He looked round the room. He could pick and choose this afternoon. The tourist season was almost at an end, thank goodness. There were a couple of blue-rinsed, Lowry-thin American women with grating accents and predatory hands. Widows, probably, he thought dispassionately, feeding on the carrion of well-insured husbands. One of them had the extraordinarily taut, characterless features that betrayed multiple face-lifts but the liver-spotted hands gave her age away. Three well-dressed, comfortably-off county ladies had their heads together under the watchful guard of the plaster nymphs in the centre of the room, their voices, beautifully modulated but of immense carrying power, making no secret about the plans for the last gymkhana of the season. Then there was the pianist, of course. He sounded better from the other side of the room. The only other occupant was an elderly grey-haired woman who looked preoccupied. Linus sat at the next table with his back to the jade-green wallpaper. He always felt safer with his back to the wall and a broad view of the room in front and suspected there was something very primitive in such a feeling.

The waitress took his order and his glance took in the woman at the next table. There was something vaguely—very vaguely—familiar about her. He worried the familiarity about in his mind for a while but was unable to put it out of its misery so he got up and fetched one of the newspapers from the hook on the wall. This was the only place he knew where newspapers in continental-style wooden holders were available for guests.

The elderly woman glanced up at him as he passed her table and Linus smiled absent-mindedly, as one does to strangers with whom one has no particular desire to fall into conversation. She smiled back equally absent-mindedly and then frowned. As he read his paper and waited for his tea, he was aware of her surreptitious scrutiny. It made him feel uncomfortable.

There's something compulsive about being stared at and it was probably inevitable that he should find himself returning the scrutiny. Finally she spoke.

'Young man,' she said, beckoning to him and Linus, irresistibly reminded of the wedding-guest and the Ancient Mariner, obeyed the signal. 'Young man,' she reiterated, 'do you know me?'

Linus felt as self-conscious as any schoolboy caught peering through a keyhole despite the fact that the scrutiny had been a two-way affair.

'I'm not sure,' he said. 'There's something familiar about you but I must admit I haven't been able to pin it down.' He hoped his apologetic tone sounded sincere. It is, after all, rather insulting not to be able to remember someone.

'Yes,' she said. 'If you're who I think you are, you always were a polite boy.' She studied him frankly. 'The beard doesn't help, of course.'

Linus instinctively fingered the George-V-and-Tsar-Nicholas he affected, in part to hide old scars. 'You seem to be further ahead than I am,' he told her. 'Perhaps you'd put me out of my misery.'

She shook her head. 'No. It's important that you identify me for yourself. Important to me, that is,' she added, catching his startled expression.

'I see,' Linus said, though he didn't. 'Do the rules of the game allow you to give me a clue?'

The waitress appeared with Linus's tray and the woman gestured to her to put it on her table. The girl looked a question-mark at Linus and he nodded.

'I don't see why not,' the woman said when the waitress had gone. 'It was a long time ago. About thirty years.

Perhaps a little less. You were at veterinary college—at least, you were if you're who I think you are.'

That seemed fairly conclusive and it focused Linus's concentration most effectively. He made an intelligent guess. 'Were you a friend of my mother's?'

She nodded.

A friend of his mother's when he was at college. He had a sudden image of a sandy-coloured dog. 'I know,' he exclaimed. 'You let me palpate one of your bitches to see if she was in whelp. "One of". You must have had several. I remember now—you had some weird and wonderful breed that no one had ever heard of and you lived . . . oh, in the north of the county somewhere. It began with an S. Shotteswell? No. Shottington. Lower Shottington. But I'm sorry, I'm afraid the name eludes me completely.'

The woman seemed very slightly to have relaxed. 'That weird and wonderful breed was the Antiguan Truffle Dog, if that helps,' she contributed.

Linus wasn't sure that it did but nevertheless he found himself coming up with a name. 'Enid?' he tried. 'No, that's not quite right. Edith. Yes, that's it.' Everything slipped into place then. 'Edith Ledwell. You gave up the dogs to go to Australia with your husband. Wasn't he ill or something?' He suddenly remembered that Ralph Ledwell had been quite a bit older than his wife and this woman was no spring chicken. Her husband must almost certainly be dead by now. 'I'm sorry,' he said. 'That was thoughtless of me. I imagine you're a widow.'

She smiled, not unkindly. 'Only for about a year. The move did Ralph the world of good. That isn't important. What matters is that you do recognize me? You really do?'

Her intensity was disconcerting. 'Yes, of course,' he said. 'I recognized you straight away. It was just nailing it down that was difficult.'

She leant back in the sofa, with an audible exhalation of

relief. 'Thank goodness for that!' she said. 'You've no idea how you've cheered me up. I feel almost normal again.'

Linus was unsure whether he was expected to press for clarification of such comments which, mundane enough in themselves, became cryptic in this particular context. The worst he could do was offend her but she had laid herself open to that by raising the matter and there was no denying the fact that he was mildly intrigued. A small enigma lightened a disappointing day. 'You must have known hundreds of people in this area,' he remarked. 'Why should the recognition of one of them cause such overwhelming relief?'

She hesitated. 'I don't think you want to be bothered with an old woman's story, and besides, it's rather peculiar.'

'I've plenty of time and I've only just begun my tea,' Linus told her, pouring some out as if to confirm this. He guessed from her demeanour that she was really quite anxious to tell whatever it was to someone and it might as well be he. 'I like peculiar stories,' he added.

So, while Linus munched his way through a delicate assortment of sandwiches, she told him what she had found at Perry Park. 'It was all very disturbing,' she concluded.

'So I imagine,' Linus said, spreading the butter sufficiently thickly on his scone to leave teethmarks when he bit into it. 'And you can think of no explanation?'

'None at all, and I can promise you I've thought of little else since then. It wasn't just the name—or the address or the breed, come to that. Any one of them would have been unusual, any two would have been explicable as a coincidence, but not all three and especially not when appearance is added to it.'

'Was there so great a resemblance, then?' Linus asked.

Edith Ledwell considered that carefully. 'I suppose not, really. I mean, if we were identically dressed, I don't think anyone would have the slightest difficulty telling us apart. On the other hand, we're very much the same age and build and if someone hadn't seen either of us for twenty years, one of us could easily be taken for the other.'

'You said she had a son. Is that another similarity?'

'No. Ralph and I had no children at all.'

'He'd be about my age, I suppose,' Linus said. He was not looking forward to the prospect of fifty. 'Not that that's likely to be relevant. It sounds to me as if she must have done it purely and simply to trade on your established name and reputation. Is there a lot of money to be made in that breed?'

'If there were, I could understand it. In the old days the bitches came into season just once in alternate years and produced on average just one puppy. It was a very odd breed in that respect. Now I gather they breed once a year and may have as many as four in a litter but, even so, it's not a recipe for printing money. It looks as if they're much easier to sell nowadays, if the numbers being exhibited are anything to go by, but I can't imagine the most successful breeder does more than cover costs.'

Linus nodded. That made sense. It seemed pointless for anyone to go to all the trouble of acquiring someone else's name, home, affix and breed just to build on an existing reputation when what created the reputation was presumably the quality of the dogs—and that, according to Mrs Ledwell, was good enough to have built the breeder's reputation no matter what she had called herself. It was very puzzling.

'I take it you'd have no difficulty proving who you are?' he asked.

'I suppose not.' She seemed surprised. 'I've got my passport, of course, and I suppose my birth and marriage certificates are obtainable. I didn't think to bring the originals to England with me.'

'One wouldn't,' Linus agreed and refrained from pointing out that the other Mrs Ledwell would have had no difficulty obtaining copies of the relevant papers in order to support her claim. 'I was thinking about proving who you were to the Kennel Club. You must have some sort of letter or certificate granting you your affix in the first place?'

'I must have had one,' she said doubtfully. 'In fact, I'm fairly sure I did, but where it is now, I've no idea. I can't even remember if I bothered to take it with me when we emigrated.'

Linus was thoughtful. 'I can see how distressing this must be for you,' he said at last. 'You must have felt as if you suddenly didn't exist, but are there any implications beyond the purely canine? Are there insurance policies or trust-fund income that she could appropriate with your name?'

'No, nothing like that. There were no inheritances likely, nothing.'

'All the same, it might be worth while to hire someone to look into that aspect: there's an outside possibility someone left you something worth the fraud.'

She shook her head. 'We were comfortably off but we didn't move in that sort of circle. I suppose it's conceivable that someone might have left me a set of teaspoons or their doggy scrapbooks, but that's as far as it would go.'

'In that case, you need to ask yourself whether you want to do anything about the deception. It must be possible to lodge some sort of complaint with the Kennel Club.'

'I've thought about it—and I very nearly did, at the show. But I asked myself why? What would be the point? If I were going to go back into dogs seriously, that would be different. Then I'd fight tooth and nail to get my own affix—my own identity, for that matter—back. As it is, the whole situation makes me feel very uneasy but I keep asking myself if it really matters and the simple answer is that it can't do.'

Linus poured himself another cup of tea and stirred the milk in punctiliously before responding. 'If it makes you uneasy, it matters,' he said. 'Would you like me to root around and see what I can find out?'

'Would you?' She smiled gratefully. 'Wouldn't it be a dreadful imposition? It would be quite a relief to feel that someone was going to get to the bottom of it but it's an awful nerve to ask an almost complete stranger to do so.'

'Nonsense,' Linus said gallantly. 'We'll call it a small return for having been allowed to manhandle your valuable bitches in a very inexpert manner all those years ago. Besides,' he added truthfully, 'I'm not at all sure I'm going to find out anything of any real use. I'm not even sure where to begin.'

CHAPTER 3

It wasn't the beginning that proved difficult. He escorted Edith Ledwell back to her flat in Norham Road and as soon as he got back to his own cottage on Osney Island, he fed Ishmael, his devoted Pit Bull Terrier, made a mug of coffee and sat down in the sitting-room with a road-map and the Yellow Pages. He found Lower Shottington and set about locating the veterinary practices which the other Mrs Ledwell was most likely to patronize. Veterinary ethics naturally precluded a discussion of another vet's clients, but it was surprising how much one could learn over a friendly pint, especially when, as a government vet, there could be no suspicion of 'poaching' clients. He decided to start with David Thelwall, who had a large quarantine kennel and a small practice—the one a direct consequence of the other—in the area. It was about due for an inspection so next morning, having registered his presence and his intentions at Government Buildings, he drove over to the disused airfield where the kennels was situated.

David Thelwall was a young man who had had the good sense to marry a wealthy farmer's daughter, a girl with a common-sense, unsentimental attitude towards animals and an inbred acceptance of the unpalatable fact that anything involving livestock also involved long hours and hard work. Just the sort of girl Linus himself should have married, he thought without rancour as he rang the bell in the perimeter fence.

The inspection of the kennels and its records was straightforward and, though time-consuming, not particularly onerous and the offer of a cup of coffee in the rather ugly brick bungalow where the Thelwalls lived was both expected and accepted. Thelwall asked after Ishmael and Ruth tried to persuade Linus that what his household needed to be complete was a kitten from the litter one of their cats was raising in the barn. Since Linus knew a kitten would last about five seconds from the time Ishmael caught sight of it, he had no difficulty in good-humouredly declining the offer and, since Ruth was equally aware of the dog's propensities, she knew there was no point in pressing her case.

'I came across a very odd woman the other day,' Linus said. 'Don't know if you know her. Lives in Lower Shottington. Ledwell. Edith Ledwell, I believe. Has Antiguan Truffle Dogs. Not one of yours, I suppose?'

Thelwall shook his head. 'Out of my radius, though I think I've heard the name.'

'I know her,' Ruth interjected. 'I used to date a boy from Shottington. She lived across the road. Fireaway Cottage, it was called. A sweet old lady but not your typical dog-breeder, if you know what I mean.'

Linus said he didn't. 'Perhaps you'd care to define your terms,' he suggested.

'I'm not sure that I can. I'm not even sure I know why I said that.' She thought about it for some minutes. 'I think it's because her interest in dogs seemed to stop short at Trufflers, as she called them. She was very knowledgeable about them but she never cross-referenced to another breed. Most dog-breeders say things like, "of course, you don't have that trouble with Shelties", or "I don't know whether you find Cavaliers do that", so that there's a perpetual building up and exchange of information. But not with Mrs Ledwell. It's as if Truffle Dogs are all there is.'

'Has she been there a long time?'

'I think so. Bill's mother—Bill was the boyfriend,' she explained self-consciously. 'She said she'd moved away—emigrated, I think—and when she came back, she persuaded the people who had her old cottage to sell it back to her. Made them an offer they couldn't refuse, I gather. Bill's mother said they didn't really want to move but the combination of a very high price and the fact that she was so anxious to move back to the house where she'd been so happy tipped the balance.'

'Hmm.' Linus cast his mind back to 'his' Mrs Ledwell's story. He remembered her to have said that the house had come on the market. Perhaps it was just a different emphasis. He'd have to ask her when he saw her. 'So she lives alone and copes with all these dogs,' he commented. 'That must be quite a task. I gather she's no youngster.'

'Now that *is* odd,' Ruth said. 'Of course, she'd been there a few years before I started going out with Bill and at that time there was a man she referred to as her son living there, but he'd joined her not all that long before. No reason why he shouldn't, of course, but apparently she hadn't had any children when they'd lived there before. The village blessed him. He worked for British Telecom and it meant they got their phones repaired pretty pronto.'

'Maybe they started a family when they were abroad,' her husband suggested.

'It's possible,' Ruth said doubtfully, 'though she must have been nearly past it when they went and even then, this one didn't look old enough.'

'Perhaps they adopted him overseas,' Linus offered.

'Probably. In fact, come to think of it, Bill's mother said something of the sort. Said he didn't look much like either his mother or his father and muttered something about changelings. Adoption is much more likely. Bill's mother was a bit like that—always reading Dark Doings into everything.'

That seam appeared to have been picked clean, so Linus finished his coffee without undue haste and took his leave.

Instead of heading back into Oxford, he turned the car

northwards towards Lower Shottington. He cruised slowly through the village, grateful for once for the thirty-mile-an-hour speed limit and located Fireaway Cottage. It was quite a small cottage of the local stone, neatly thatched and with a tidy, well-tended garden of a rather suburban type. He suspected that the neatly mown verges outside would sport daffodils and wallflowers in spring. Nice, but an anachronism. The cottage stood in a disproportionately large plot, possibly a third of an acre: unusual in these days when village gardens were sold off for building plots, but the row of kennels at the back, just visible from the road, explained that. A dog-breeder would rather have land than money any day.

There was no Post Office in the village but an old man told him where the nearest one was, at the same time indulging in a diatribe against an unspecified 'them' who closed village schools, shops and Post Offices on the assumption that everyone was born with a car in his mouth these days. Linus sympathized with the sentiment and escaped as soon as he could.

The Post Office that served Lower Shottington was fortunately too busy for the post-mistress to offer to help him find whoever it was he was looking up on the relevant electoral roll and Linus saw no good reason to enlighten her. Edith May Ledwell was the only registered occupant of Fireaway Cottage and she was too old for Jury Service. Neither piece of information was unexpected but the omission of the son's particulars was interesting, if not necessarily significant. Either he didn't live there or for some reason he chose to disenfranchise himself. It was illegal not to register and Linus knew enough about village life to be sure someone would have spotted the omission and reported it if he did live with his mother. It was quite possible he lived elsewhere in the village. Linus kicked himself for not having thought of this when he had the roll in his hands. He debated whether to go back for another look and decided against it. Such interest as he had already aroused would probably die quite quickly. If he went back it was a safe bet that every inhabitant of Lower Shottington would be told about the bearded man with a scarred face searching through their population list.

When he got back to Government Buildings, he made out his report on Thelwall's kennels and filed it. Then, after a few moments' thought, he picked up the phone and put a call through to the environmental health department of the council that served Lower Shottington. He rang in his official capacity and the girl who answered the phone found nothing unusual in his inquiry. Yes, they knew Mrs Ledwell and Fireaway Cottage. Yes, she had a breeding licence—an open one, as a matter of fact. No, there had never been any complaints about the dogs.

Linus replaced the phone. It was a pity breeders' licences hadn't been in operation before the Ledwells emigrated. There would have been a signature to compare. He rang 'his' Mrs Ledwell and told her he had made a beginning. 'There's not much to report,' he went on, 'but I'd like to have a chat.' She invited him round for a meal the following evening. Linus accepted the invitation and thought she sounded more cheerful than she had when he had first met her.

He nearly popped into Thornton's to buy her some chocolates but then it occurred to him that an elderly lady in a gardenless flat might prefer flowers so he went to the florist's instead. He wasn't much of a hand at buying flowers and sought the florist's advice.

'An elderly lady, you say? Chrysanths are very nice now. I'd suggest pink and pale mauve with the odd touch of white.'

Linus grimaced. 'Sounds horribly anæmic.' He nodded towards some tiger-lilies. 'That's a nice colour.'

The girl looked doubtful. 'I suppose we could do "autumn tints". It would be quite appropriate, really. With a touch of scarlet to liven it up, perhaps?'

Linus knew nothing about flower-arranging but he had an excellent eye for colour. He shuddered. 'A soft yellow, maybe. No scarlet.' When he came back just before closing time to collect the bouquet, he was more pleased with the result than he had expected to be. Someone had had the imagination to arrange the flowers against a background of copper beech, and the spikes of out-of-season gladioli contrasted well with the soft roundness of the chrysanthemums, while tiger-lilies lifted the whole out of the ordinary. It was certainly not anæmic. Striking would be a more apt description. 'I like it,' he said.

The girl leant across the counter conspiratorially. 'So do we. We weren't wild about the colour scheme—the soft pinks and mauves are all the things at the moment, you know—but when it was done, it made everything else look washed out by comparison.'

Edith Ledwell was delighted. 'How thoughtful!' she said. 'People so rarely bring flowers these days. It's always chocolates or wine and, with no garden of my own, flowers are particularly acceptable.' He heard her rooting around in a kitchen cupboard and then she emerged with the bouquet safely arranged in a discreetly cream vase. She stood it on a side-table, against the wall. 'There's something about a bouquet,' she remarked. 'It's quite different from a bunch of flowers, however nice they are. A bouquet makes one feel just that little bit special.'

The comment was entirely spontaneous and Linus filed it for future reference.

She poured him a whisky and herself a gin-and-tonic and when Linus was comfortably settled, she asked him what progress he had made.

'Very limited,' he admitted and told her what he had

found out. 'There is one thing that puzzles me. I thought you said that the other Mrs Ledwell had told you Fireaway Cottage had come on the market and she'd been lucky enough to be able to snap it up.'

'That's right. It was being able to get hold of her—or rather, my—old cottage that decided her to go back into Trufflers.'

'Local gossip is a bit different,' Linus said and repeated Ruth Thelwall's version of accounts. 'It's not the sort of thing that arises out of pure speculation,' he went on. 'Obviously the then owners told their neighbours all about it. After all, it's not every day someone comes along and offers you over the odds for your house. It puts a rather different complexion on her story, though, doesn't it?'

'It almost looks as if getting Fireaway Cottage was an essential part of her plan, whatever that might be,' Edith agreed.

'Which in turn suggests that being Edith Ledwell and having Antiguan Truffle Dogs and taking up the lapsed use of your affix was also part of her plan. Having the same address would clinch it, wouldn't it? If anyone queried it at that stage, they could be told that you'd decided to let it instead of selling it. I don't suppose anyone did query it—until you asked about it the other day.'

'By which time she's been there several years and the facts might well be considered uncheckable,' Edith commented.

'Which is interesting in itself,' Linus pointed out. 'Anyone who's ever lived in a village for any length of time knows that there is always at least one, and more likely several, people who will have assembled in their own minds every single fragment of information relating to everything that happens in the village which, if approached in the right manner or by the right person, they can be induced to recall. Now the one thing I particularly noticed is that the garden of that cottage is a townsman's garden: all neat lawns with trimmed edges and bedding-plants. Not unattractive in its way but very suburban, very bourgeois.'

Edith Ledwell smiled briefly. 'I'm sure your diagnosis is correct, but where does it get us? We know she's not the real Edith Ledwell and, frankly, it seems preposterous that anyone should go to so much trouble just to make a name for themselves in dogs—a name which, to judge by the quality of dogs, she'd have made anyway.'

Linus drained his glass. 'I know. It doesn't make sense. That's what bothers me.'

She leant over and patted his hand before rising from her chair. 'Never mind: I've an idea or two of my own, but let's eat first.'

She was a good cook though not, perhaps, of international reknown, and Linus was an appreciative diner, so the brandied grapefruit, the duck with morello cherries and the crowdie, with a ripe Stilton to follow, disappeared in a silence punctuated only with commendatory remarks from the guest and appropriate rejoinders from the hostess.

They took their coffee over to the sofa and settled themselves comfortably.

'I'm glad our paths crossed,' Edith told him. 'You've no idea how much it raised my spirits to meet someone who really did recognize me.'

'You certainly seem more cheerful.'

'I am. I was very depressed about it and more than a little frightened, as much as anything because I didn't understand it. I still don't, of course, but I've stopped doubting my own existence.'

'Come now, you're too sensible to exaggerate like that,' Linus told her. 'You must have met other people since your return who knew you before. Old friends who weren't connected with dogs, for instance.'

'Of course I have, though not as many as you might suppose. People don't live indefinitely. The difference between them and you is that in every single case it was I who made the approach. I identified myself to them and they accepted it. No reason why they shouldn't, of course. When it came to you, once I was sure you were Deirdre Rintoul's boy, I deliberately left it for *you* to decide who I was. That's what makes the difference.'

It would, Linus thought. He tried to imagine what it must be like to discover someone else in your shoes. A sort of doppelganger going around, pretending to be you. Very nasty. Very Hammer horror. No wonder she had been so glad to make his acquaintance.

'You said you had an idea or two of your own,' he reminded her.

'That's right. I'm going to call her bluff.'

'Complain to the Kennel Club about the unauthorized use of your affix?'

'Not at this stage. I'm going back into dogs. Truffle Dogs.'

'I thought you'd decided you were too old to start again,' Linus said doubtfully.

'That's right. Now I've changed my mind.'

Linus looked around the small, neat living-room. 'Is that entirely wise?' he asked.

'Not here. It's too small and, anyway, animals are forbidden. I can easily afford to buy a little house somewhere. I've already furnished estate agents with my requirements. Details should be dropping through my letter-box from tomorrow on.'

'Have you considered what the effect may be on your namesake?'

'Considerable disquiet, I hope,' she said with satisfaction. 'Of course, I'm not starting with my real name.'

'Does that mean you're making one up or using someone else's?'

'Someone else's.'

'That reduces you to the same level as The Other One,' Linus pointed out.

'I know, but it's only temporary and, in any case, it's too late to do anything about it because I've already done it.'

Linus was beginning to feel he had got enmeshed in something that was going to be far more devious than he liked. 'You'd better tell me what you've done,' he suggested guardedly.

'Don't look so worried,' she said, shrewdly assessing his thoughts. 'I went through the catalogue and found that about a dozen affixes were represented in Trufflers, but that two of them predominated. One was mine, the other belonged to a Mrs Warwick. Knowing the dog game, I calculated that it was a fairly safe bet they were not averse to scoring points over each other. I rang Mrs Warwick and said I was interested in getting re-started in the breed; that I liked her dogs and wondered if she had anything that might suit me. As I expected, it was the word "re-started" that sparked her interest and that interest sharpened considerably when I said it had been twenty-odd years ago—I wasn't too specific about the year—since I had had one. "Oh," she said. "You must have known Edith Ledwell." I agreed that I had and managed without actually saying so to convey the suggestion that it wasn't something I much liked being reminded of. I told her I was Ilse Trautgarden.'

'Good grief!' Linus exclaimed.

'Yes, I know—most improbable name but it has the merit of being unforgettable.'

'Is it real?'

'Absolutely. Ilse's name will be in a lot of the old catalogues, if anyone has them, and in the old dog Annuals. We were very good friends, as a matter of fact, but she went out of dogs soon after I emigrated—a couple of years after, I think. She developed Parkinson's disease. There wasn't much they could do about it in those days and she died about ten years ago but she'd had nothing at all to do with dogs since she gave them up. Mrs Warwick has a litter in the nest and she says although it's early days, there's a little girl there that may turn out very nicely and if I'm really serious, she'll consider letting me jump the queue because her other bookings are mostly for pets. Which means she hasn't got enough bookings to cover the whole litter,' Edith added with some asperity.

'Cynic.'

'Realist.'

'Isn't it going to create problems if you go to see these puppies—as I presume you intend to do sooner or later—as Ilse Trautgarden and then reveal at some stage that you're another Edith Ledwell? Discovery of an alias is generally an indication of criminal intent. I wouldn't sell you a dog if you pulled that one on me.'

'You would if you had a litter to sell,' Edith said confidently. 'Besides, I don't think I'll tell her until after I've bought it. I don't want the phone lines buzzing until after I've appeared in the ring. Then she can think what she likes.'

Linus regarded her with surprised respect. Edith Ledwell was revealing unexpected strengths. The little old lady who had been so uncertain of herself at their first encounter had retrieved her personality along with her identity. He cast his mind back to his student days. This present image was much closer to the one he had known. He had attributed her more diffident aspect to her age and her bereavement. Now he realized it was an indication that the shock of discovering a pretender had been deeper than he had thought.

'So what happens now?' he asked.

'I can't see that anything does for the next couple of weeks. Then I'm going up to Mrs Warwick's to look at these puppies. There's no point in looking at them yet. I want to see them running around.'

'Would you like me to come with you?' Linus asked, half hoping the offer would be declined.

'I'd like you to take me,' she said. 'I don't drive any more and almost nowhere these days can be reached by public transport.'

'What do you want to do about your alter ego in the meantime?' he asked.

'I don't see that there's much I can do, do you? I'd like to know why this mysteriously acquired son—who is, you realize, the only point at which she appears to differ from me—doesn't appear on the electoral roll.'

'We don't know that,' Linus corrected. 'Only that he doesn't live with his mother. He may very well live somewhere else in the village—or even in another village.'

She shook her head. 'We can discount another village. She said he helped her with the dogs. Shottington is often cut off in winter, so he wouldn't always be able to get through. No, my guess is he lives in the same village. I'll go into County Hall and look at the electoral roll there. That won't occasion comment. You might keep your ears open as you go around the county and see if you can glean anything.'

'You realize that if the national papers get hold of this, they'll have a field day,' Linus warned.

'Let them. I've nothing to hide. It could be quite useful. In fact, come to think of it, if I can't get to the bottom of it with your help, I may very well bring them in to root around.'

Linus mulled this over with some distaste. 'If you're right about this Mrs Warwick needing to sell her puppies, what happens if someone else comes along ready to buy? Won't that leave you high and dry?'

She shook her head. 'She'll ring me. I left her my phone

number—just the code and the number: I don't want her knowing it's Oxford and looking Ilse Trautgarden up in the phone book only to find there isn't one.'

Linus stood up to go. 'That was a delicious meal, Mrs Ledwell. Perhaps you'd allow me to return the compliment. Let me take you to lunch on Sunday?'

'I'd love it. It always seems so pointless to make Sunday lunch for one person.'

'I'll pick you up about half past twelve,' he said.

As he drove the short distance back to Osney Island, Linus berated himself for getting involved, though it was difficult to see how he could have avoided it. He was committed to taking Mrs Ledwell over to Mrs Warwick—and goodness only knew where she lived, because Linus hadn't thought to ask—but then, even if Mrs Ledwell bought a puppy, it would be months before she could take it to a dog show. He wasn't sure what the bottom age limit was, but he was sure there was one and, by the time Mrs Ledwell's projected puppy reached it, he might well have been able to slip quietly out of the picture. Her improved spirits gave every indication that she was more than capable of dealing without his help with anything her substitute might choose to throw at her.

CHAPTER 4

Sunday's weather was glorious and Linus took Ishmael for a good long walk along the towpath after breakfast. There were still holiday-makers' cabin cruisers tied up along the bank, curtains tightly drawn, wasting the best hours of the day, in Linus's opinion. He was definitely a morning-man himself. They both enjoyed the walk and it crossed Linus's mind—not for the first time—that retirement, when it came, might have distinct compensations.

Mrs Ledwell had rung him the previous day and suggested that he might like coffee before they went out, so he timed leaving Osney rather earlier than he had originally intended and reached Norham Road not very long after eleven. A small car park served the flats but he chose to park outside and thus avoid the chance of unwittingly taking some other tenant's place. He rang the bell and positioned himself in line with the peephole so that Edith Ledwell would be able to identify him before she opened the door. The door remained closed.

He rang again and this time put his ear to the lock. He was sure he could hear something inside. It sounded as if it might be the radio. Obviously she hadn't heard the bell. He put his finger on it and kept it there for an appreciable time. Still no answer. Mrs Ledwell hadn't struck him as being deaf but some impairment to her hearing—entirely to be expected at seventy-two—and the radio might explain that, especially if she had closed the door between the living-room and the little hall. He looked at his watch. Quarter past eleven. Surely she must be expecting him by now? He rang the bell once more and then, when it still wasn't answered, went outside again. Thank goodness it was a ground-floor flat. No one liked finding someone peering through their windows, not even if that someone was an expected visitor, but a bang on the window ought to attract the attention the bell had not.

He stepped over the lavender that bordered the drive, ignoring the small, discreet 'Keep Off' signs in the lawn. Each ground-floor flat had a small paved area outside the french windows of the living-room. Linus guessed it was referred to as a patio. Some tenants had livened theirs up with tubs of flowers but Edith Ledwell hadn't bothered, probably because she didn't regard the flat as a permanent home.

Linus briefly checked the outside of the building with his knowledge of the inside lay-out. He had no intention of startling one of the other residents if a little care could avoid it. No wonder she hadn't heard the bell. The french windows were partly open, allowing in all the noise from the street —the occasional car, the frequent child on its way with its friends to the adjacent parks—to compete with the radio which, from here, was quite loud. He crossed the grass and as soon as he stepped on to the paving, stopped short. One of the panes, the one beside the handle, was broken.

He glanced into the room. A heavy lamp had been knocked on to the floor from the low coffee-table on which it had stood. The cream vase had been knocked over and the bouquet scattered. Drawers had been emptied and their contents strewn. In short, even to Linus's untutored eye, the room bore all the signs of a burglary. He opened the french window wider and stepped in.

There wasn't much doubt about it. If the police didn't already know, they'd better be told, but Edith Ledwell's well-being was more important first. He stepped carefully over the debris and put his head round the door leading into the long, narrow galley-like kitchen. Items had been strewn about here, too, but there was no sign of Mrs Ledwell.

Linus told himself that she was probably with a neighbour and had simply forgotten all about his intended visit but in the pit of his stomach was a nasty presentiment that that was too easy. The living-room door was closed, as he had suspected from the outside. He opened it and went into the hall. All the rooms off this were closed. The first revealed an undisturbed bathroom. The room next to the bathroom would be the smaller of the two bedrooms. He would try the one opposite first.

Edith Ledwell was still in bed but one glance at the battered pulp that had been her head and the blood-bespattered room, told Linus she must be dead. All the same, his veterinary instincts demanded proof and he pulled the covers back to feel her pulse. It proved unnecessary. Rigor mortis had set in, so not only was she dead, but she had been for some time. He looked around. This room, too, bore the signs of a hasty search. Then his stomach took over and he rushed to the bathroom.

After that, he dialled 999 and poured himself a very stiff whisky while he waited. In a way, he was glad there was nothing he could do for his mother's old friend, because he didn't think he could bear to go back into that room again. Belatedly, he thought about things like evidence and fingerprints, and took his drink into the hall where he stood awkwardly, not touching anything, until the police arrived.

Two of them were in plain clothes. 'Touched anything, have we, sir?' one of these asked.

Linus nodded. 'I'm afraid so—quite a lot. I didn't think. Not at first. All the doors—except the other bedroom. The telephone, of course. The bedclothes. Oh, and I switched the radio off. I couldn't stand the banal noise.'

'It was on when you came, was it?' Linus nodded. 'Did you change the station before you switched it off—search for something more to your taste?'

Linus shook his head, and the policeman recorded that fact.

'Tell me, sir, why did you interfere with the bedclothes?'

'I didn't "interfere" with them. I pulled them back. I intended to take her pulse but it wasn't necessary. Rigor mortis had set in.'

'I'm surprised you should have bothered, given the state of her head,' the policeman commented.

'I'm a vet, Officer. You don't assume death, you prove it. Rigor mortis proves it very conclusively but it wasn't apparent at first—the bedclothes were up to her shoulders. It was as if she had been bludgeoned while she slept.'

'Detective as well, I see.' He wrote something more in his notebook. 'Is there anything else you touched, sir?'

'No, I don't think so. If I recall anything, I'll tell you.'

The policeman's eyes travelled to the glass in Linus's hand. 'The whisky just materialized, did it, sir?' he said with heavy politeness.

'No, of course not,' Linus said tetchily. 'I forgot it, that's all. I picked up the bottle and the glass—and it was kept in that sideboard over there, so I touched the door-handle. The door, too, I expect. One doesn't think.'

'Obviously. We'll have to take your fingerprints, then, so that we know which ones to eliminate. Is there anything that strikes you as missing?'

'Anything stolen, you mean?' Linus looked around. 'Nothing that I remember, but I've only been here once before.'

'So you're not an old friend of Mrs Ledwell's?'

'I barely know her. She was a friend of my mother's. She and her husband emigrated to Australia and she's just returned. We bumped into each other in the Randolph the other day. I was taking her out to lunch.' He remembered the booked table. 'I'd better ring the Bay Tree and cancel.'

'The Bay Tree, was it?' the policeman said, noting that

fact. 'I don't think you need bother. We'll be in touch with them later on. I'm sure they'll understand.'

At the Police Station they took his fingerprints and asked a lot more questions before finally taking a statement from him. From the drift of their questions Linus concluded that they were trying to find out whether he was in sufficiently dire financial straits to make it worth his while to murder an elderly, and possibly wealthy, widow.

'If I'd wanted to murder her, I could have found several less brutal methods. I am a vet, you know, with all the access that implies to drugs designed for euthanasia. In fact, it might be easier for a vet than for a doctor: they're not supposed to put their patients down. We do it all the time.'

'So you'd take very good care not to use one of those methods, wouldn't you, sir? You wouldn't want to draw attention to yourself.'

Linus decided after that to keep his mouth shut except for straight answers to their questions and found that things moved far more easily when he adopted that policy. He was signing his statement when the door opened and Inspector Lacock came in. Linus would not have described the Inspector as a friend, but they were reasonably well acquainted and he was pleased to see a familiar face. Linus's conscience was completely clear where Edith Ledwell's death was concerned but there was no denying several hours in a police station, quite isolated from 'ordinary' folk, was a confidence-shaking experience.

'I heard you were here,' the Inspector said. 'They say it looks like a vicious attack by a burglar.'

Linus nodded. 'That's what I took it to be. She must have woken up when they—or he—was rifling through the bedroom drawers.'

'Sounds reasonable. I suppose you were safely tucked up in bed at the time?'

'If the time they've fixed for her death is right, then, yes.'

'Alone?'

'Unfortunately.'

Inspector Lacock permitted himself the indulgence of a smile. 'In more senses than one, I imagine. Pity you're not married.'

'I can think of many reasons for getting married, Inspector,' Linus said. 'The off-chance it might provide an alibi some time is about the worst.'

He went home when they'd finished with him and it wasn't until his own front door closed behind him that the shock symptoms manifested themselves. He made himself some hot, sweet tea, which he loathed and had to force down, and then laced it with brandy in an attempt to make it palatable. He turned on the television but its Sunday-evening banalities couldn't engage his mind and neither could the book he took up instead. He finally decided that the only thing to do, early as it was, was to go to bed and he made doubly sure every window-catch and door-lock was secure before he retired. He didn't want to be alone, either, so Ishmael, much to his surprise, was brought upstairs to curl up on the carpet at the foot of his master's bed. At least, that was Linus's intention and that was how it started out but Ishmael felt it was a situation that could be improved upon and in the morning he was curled up on the end of the bed. It took a long time before Linus fell asleep. Every time he closed his eyes, Edith Ledwell's battered head emerged against the closed lids and even when he did finally lose consciousness, his dreams took the day's unprecedented events and wove them into a surrealist evocation of his daily work. Ritual slaughterers killed beasts with Edith Ledwell's face and plainclothes policemen prodded cattle at the Banbury stockyards.

Linus awoke late, less exhausted but scarcely refreshed and decided the Government could manage without him for a day. He turned on breakfast television and there was a brief reference to the murder in the local news. No mention was made of the identity of the person who discovered the body. It was a day of desultory activity with only a visit from the local paper to make him concentrate his mind.

'I'd rather you didn't mention my name,' he said, without much hope. 'I'm just a friend of the poor soul—not even that, really—and I can do without the ghoulish questions of every Tom, Dick and Harry who half knows me.'

'I know what you mean,' the girl sympathized. 'I'll see what I can do. The police don't seem to think you're very important, so maybe the editor will let it through without naming you. I can't promise anything, mind.'

She was as good as her word, though, and when the evening paper came out he was only referred to as 'a long-standing friend'. If the paper was to be believed, the police were quite sure the murder had been an impulse killing in the course of a burglary. They were, naturally, appealing for witnesses. Linus didn't think their chances of finding anyone who saw anything in Norham Road in the early hours were very great.

He went to work the next day but found it hard to concentrate. The shock and numbness were beginning to wear off and to be replaced with anger. The unnecessary loss of a life had always angered him. When he had been in general practice, it had always annoyed him to have to put down perfectly healthy animals for no other reason than that their owners had found some excuse for not keeping them. He used to tell himself that it was much better they should be put down than just abandoned, but it still jarred. The unnecessary death of an old lady was much worse and he began to wonder if there had been some way in which he could have foreseen the possibility and thereby perhaps have prevented it. There wasn't, and that in turn made him feel guilty.

He felt worse about it, in a way, because he knew the

business over the other Edith Ledwell had left her in a far from easy state of mind and he was the one who had undertaken to do something about it, and he had so far failed. Perhaps he could make restitution by taking up that little mystery on her behalf and solving it. If he did that, perhaps her soul would be able to rest in peace.

Linus despised himself, not for the sentiment, but for the imagery in which he instinctively set it. It was half superstition and half religion—and some people would argue that the two were synonymous. It certainly wasn't rational. Linus had no belief in a life after death and, without that belief, what point was there in such phrases as letting souls rest in peace? Nevertheless, whatever his head told him, his emotions, his instincts, whatever one chose to call them, all told him to lay the ghost; to uncover what was almost certainly a very simple explanation and then be able to forget the whole business.

He was a bit surprised on the next Saturday to receive a visit from Inspector Lacock.

'It's not official,' the Inspector told him. 'Can I come in?'

Linus stood aside to let him. 'What do you mean, it's not official?' he said. 'It's always official where you people are concerned.'

'All right, let's say it's not ostensibly official. Will that do? I thought this might interest you. One of our dog-handlers brought it in.' He handed Linus a tabloid-sized newsprint publication: the sort that is neither paper nor magazine but somehow both. It carried a colour photo of an Afghan Hound and it was called *Dog World*. 'It's on page three. The headline is "Mistaken Identity".'

Linus obediently turned to page three. It wasn't so much an article as a letter addressed to all readers and it was from Edith Ledwell. In it she thanked all those tremendously kind people who had written and telephoned her son, Patrick, to offer their condolences on her untimely and violent death but she was happy to say, with Mark Twain, that reports of her death had been greatly exaggerated. She was alive, very well, and the unfortunate victim of that brutal attack was simply someone with the same name. She was happy to say that the resemblance ended there and she looked forward to seeing all her friends in the ring at Driffield.

'Odd coincidence,' Lacock remarked.

'Yes, very.'

'Was she in dogs, your Mrs Ledwell?'

'Not so far as I know. She had been, years ago, before she and her husband emigrated. She told me she'd had to give them up then, because she didn't have the time. She was toying with the idea of getting another one once she'd decided whether to remain here or go back to Australia. She thought it would be company for her. She was talking about getting a little mongrel from a dogs' home, then she wouldn't be tempted to show it.'

'Why should she want to avoid that temptation?' Lacock asked.

Linus shrugged. 'I got the impression she didn't much like some aspects of the game.' He handed the Inspector back his paper.

'No, keep it,' Lacock said. 'I thought that item would interest you, that's all. If you can think of any way it might tie in with the other Edith Ledwell's death, perhaps you'd let me know.'

Linus laughed briefly. 'And that's what you call an unofficial visit? I told you there was no such thing. Yes, Inspector, if I can connect her death with this coincidence, I'll let you know.'

It was something Linus thought about a lot in the ensuing days, but he could find no connection beyond the name. Even if he had good reason for suspecting—as Inspector Lacock hadn't—that the one Edith Ledwell had taken the other's identity, there was absolutely nothing to connect the substitute with the murder. In the light of the facts at his disposal, there was no possible motive, particularly since 'his' Edith Ledwell had quite deliberately not publicized her existence. Nor, despite worrying at it like a terrier in every spare moment, could he come up with a rational explanation as to why the other one should not just have adopted Mrs Ledwell's identity, but gone to so much trouble to do so. Any solution to the puzzle was going to take a lot more than academic speculation. He was going to have to do something positive or drop the matter. Linus was very tempted to take the latter course but he didn't like loose ends and, even if he didn't feel under an obligation to the dead woman, he would have felt impelled to carry on searching.

The Kennel Club gave him Mrs Warwick's telephone number and he groaned when he realized it used the Barnsley code. All the same, he rang her and said he was Mrs Trautgarden's godson and would be bringing her up to see the puppies if Mrs Warwick would like to set a date. Mrs Warwick was delighted and her directions were clear enough.

He knew Mrs Warwick had no reason to suspect there might have been two Edith Ledwells and still less to imagine that Ilse Trautgarden had any closer association with either of them than was afforded by a connection, broken twenty-five years ago, with the same kind of dog. He wondered briefly whether it would be a good idea to persuade another elderly lady to go with him and pretend to be Mrs Trautgarden. He rejected the idea. It was hardly ethical to persuade someone to act a lie and 'Mrs Trautgarden' would be expected to make intelligent noises about the breed. Besides, he didn't know any old ladies well enough to ask them. No, it would be better for his 'godmother' to be indisposed and he would dutifully keep her appointment to save inconveniencing Mrs Warwick. That way, his ignorance of the breed wouldn't matter and he could ask whatever inane questions he wanted to.

Mrs Warwick had warned him that the 'courtyard' where she lived wasn't marked on road-maps and Linus thought 'courtyard' was a strange word to use for a collection of houses right out in the country. When he got there, he found it to be an entirely accurate description. Some half-dozen or so stone houses, all roughly contemporary with each other, were clustered round a cobbled courtyard at the end of an unadopted road. Linus was no expert on Yorkshire architecture, but he guessed them to date from the eighteenth century at the latest. They were all substantial houses, excellently maintained and the sombre stone glowed in the autumn sunshine. Everything about the little enclave breathed prosperity. Linus had never seen anywhere like it and found himself quite envious of those who could afford to live here. Mrs Warwick lived at one end of the courtyard in a house that opened straight on to the cobbles but which, as he discovered when she took him into the sitting-room, stood in several acres of gardens and had the most stupendous views over a valley to the not-too-distant hills. His exclamation of admiration was spontaneous.

'It is lovely, isn't it? Mrs Warwick said, standing beside him at the bay window. 'Everyone admires it and, of course, it's a perfect place for dogs. Let me get you some coffee and we can have a chat while we drink it and then I'll show you the puppies. Do take a seat when you've admired the view enough,' and she left him temporarily to his own devices.

The coffee was the real thing and the biscuits were home-made. Linus began to be very glad he had come. Everything about the place was eroding his southerner's entrenched belief that Yorkshire meant grime, dark satanic mills and the odd bleak moor to account for the Brontës.

'I'm sorry your godmother couldn't make it,' Mrs Warwick said. 'I hope it's nothing serious.'

Death generally is, he thought. Aloud, he said, 'I hope not, too, but at her age one can't be too careful.'

'How old is she? She must be quite an age. I looked her up in some old books and it's well over twenty years since she was active in the breed.'

'To be honest, I don't know exactly,' Linus said truthfully. 'She can't be far short of eighty.'

Mrs Warwick looked worried. 'And she's thinking of having a puppy? Is that wise?'

Linus leant forward conspiratorially. 'I'm not entirely happy about it,' he admitted. 'If she must have a dog, I think she'd be better advised to have an elderly one in need of a good home. I think she's forgotten what a pain a very active puppy can be.'

The kennels were spotless, the concrete runs having the bleached appearance that comes with regular scrubbing down. The buildings themselves were the commercially produced sort that come in prefabricated sections to be erected on site, but they were all well insulated and coated with a non-toxic preservative. The dogs were well cared for and happy and seemed very fond both of their young kennelmaid and their owner.

'The puppies are over here,' Mrs Warwick said, taking him to a large kennel that stood apart, entirely surrounded by its own run, a sensible arrangement designed to minimize the risk of infection.

'You only have the one breed?' he asked.

'I've never felt the need for another,' she said. 'Trufflers are as near to the perfect companion dog as you could wish to find.'

'You've had them a long time, I take it?'

'About fifteen years.' She laughed. 'As a matter of fact, that's something of a bone of contention in the breed: who's been in it longest. There's a very well known Truffle Dog breeder called Edith Ledwell. I don't know if you know her?'

Linus replied, with perfect truth, that he thought he had heard the name.

'Your godmother will know her. She introduced the breed but then she emigrated. I came into Trufflers when she was abroad and about five years after that, she returned, so there's always been a bit of rivalry as to who has been associated with the breed longest. She likes to date it from the time she introduced them, even though she was out of them for years and years. I maintain that's cheating, and only the years she was actually *in* them counts.'

'I can see the issue could well be contentious,' Linus agreed.

'It's superficially very amicable,' Mrs Warwick told him, 'but I know it niggles her a bit and I must confess there have been times when I've rather stressed it just to bring her down to size occasionally.'

It occurred to Linus that this was first indication he had had that 'Edith Ledwell' was not a sweet old lady. Interesting, particularly since Mrs Warwick didn't strike him as a fool.

The puppies were delightful, as puppies always are and, to Linus's untutored eye, identical except in the matter of sex. Mrs Warwick saw them differently. There was one which, she said, showed signs of outstanding potential. She enthused over its coat, its eye, the proportions of its skull and its tail-set; its movement was excellent but if she really had to nitpick—and, as she was sure Linus realized, the perfect dog had yet to be born—she would like to see a *leetle* more spring of rib. She contrasted this paragon with the dog puppy, drawing Linus's attention to the latter's shortcomings. Linus looked and listened and made what he hoped were intelligent noises, but he still couldn't tell them apart.

'If your godmother wants one,' Mrs Warwick continued, 'this is the one to have. She can expect to do some good winning with this, but I'd like to know fairly quickly. I shan't have any difficulty selling her, in fact, I've got someone waiting on Mrs Trautgarden's decision as it is, and she won't wait indefinitely.'

She was obviously telling the truth and Linus felt guilty at having taken up so much of her time on what he knew had been a pointless exercise from the beginning. Since there was no possibility of a sale to Mrs Trautgarden, he couldn't allow her to risk losing a genuine one.

'If you've another buyer, then let it go,' he told her. 'Let me be quite frank with you, Mrs Warwick. My godmother says she wants one but I really don't think she'll be able to cope—not with a puppy, at any rate. And that's not all. She's been remarkably consistent about wanting another Truffler but the fact remains that her memory isn't what it was and it wouldn't surprise me at all if I mentioned it one day and she asked me what I was talking about.'

It was a convincing story and Mrs Warwick was convinced. 'It certainly sounds as if it might be wiser not to encourage her in her present intention. Are you quite sure she won't be upset if she learns I've let it go?'

'Not remotely,' Linus assured her truthfully. 'In fact, if you've no objection, I'll say none of them were quite up to the standard I know she wants.'

'None whatever, though I must say I shall be sorry not to meet her. I was only saying to someone else in the breed the other day how nice it would be to compare notes with someone from the early days. Still, life's full of little disappointments, isn't it?'

Linus agreed wholeheartedly that it was, and took his leave. He drove southwards down the M1 a great deal faster than was either wise or lawful and despised himself for having so effectively lied and half-truthed and conned a perfectly genuine woman. And all to what end? Precious little. He'd had a pleasant day out but what had he learned?

Only that Mrs Warwick was not quite the adoring admirer of Mrs Ledwell that he had begun to think was usual and that Mrs Ledwell didn't like being reminded of the break in her association with Truffle Dogs. He had also learned that Mrs Warwick had mentioned his 'godmother's' intended visit. He wondered to whom, but guessed it had not been to Mrs Ledwell. Somehow he didn't think the two ladies were on quite those terms. Mrs Warwick would have got greater satisfaction from producing 'Ilse Trautgarden' at a show—with a product of Mrs Warwick's breeding. That really would have been one in the eye for the doyenne of the breed.

He shut the front door behind him, glad, as he always was, to reach a haven that was entirely his. The woman who cleaned for him once a week had been, so everything shone and there was the old-fashioned smell of wax polish about. He put the kettle on and greeted Ishmael who, as always, was positively hyperbolic in his delight. Then, when the dog had finally been persuaded that he really did need to go in the garden, Linus filled his feeding-bowl with mixer and a tin of meat, and let Ishmael back in. It would take him five seconds flat to demolish the lot. Whoever it was who said that a dog had only four thoughts, one for each foot—food, food, sex and food—was about right, though Ishmael was obliged to sublimate the third of these.

Linus took his coffee into the sitting-room and eased himself into an armchair with a sigh of contentment and emptied his mind of the concerns of the day. On the wall beside him was one of his particular treasures and he studied it with undiminished pleasure. It was a small oil sketch by Landseer which Linus had picked up years ago when the artist was still denigrated. The dealers had described it as a Chow, though what Chow had ever been red and white, Linus had yet to learn. His intense pleasure in it came, not because of its enormously increased value, but in part for its own sake and in part because its acquisition was a silent tribute to his own powers of discrimination. Linus had been a very run-of-the-mill GP vet, though he was an efficient, if occasionally erratic, civil servant; his lack of ambition had made him—in his wife's eyes, at least—a disappointing husband and he had only recently been able to establish any sort of rapport with his son. But he did have a good eye for a picture even if he lacked the finance to indulge it to the hilt. Or maybe, he thought suddenly, because he lacked those funds. He had to be discriminating. Not only was there a limit to the money he could afford to spend, but also a limit to the wall-space in this small cottage.

Antiguan Truffle Dogs began to obtrude on dubious Chows. What did he do now? He had listened to Mrs Warwick expounding on the merits of her puppies and although he hadn't been able to pick up the subtle distinctions of which she had been so aware, he now knew what he was supposed to be looking for. He was very much afraid there was nothing for it but to tackle the other Edith Ledwell in person. He glanced across at the telephone. Not this evening. This evening he'd have something to eat, watch television and have an early night. He went out into the kitchen and rinsed out his mug, dried it and put it away. He liked things neat. He opened the freezer door but there was nothing that tempted him. He considered briefly having something that didn't and decided against it. He looked at his watch. Half past six. He'd give it an hour and then get something at the pub. He reached for his jacket and called Ishmael. A good walk would do both of them a bit of good.

CHAPTER 5

It was an odd sensation finally to meet 'Edith Ledwell'. So much time and effort had been expended on trying to assess her motives that Linus had to remind himself as he drew up outside Fireaway Cottage that they'd never met and that, although he might feel as if he knew the woman he had begun to think of as The Other One, he was a total stranger to her. She was small and thin and very erect but seemed somehow more frail than the woman she had usurped. She was neatly and tidily dressed but with no regard for colour or style, rather as if she had put on the first clean garments to come to hand. Nevertheless, the broad physical similarities were such that the immediate impression was of an uncanny similarity to the late Mrs Ledwell. Linus was quite sure that if he had not seen either of them for twenty years, he would have taken either for the other and attributed such differences as there were to the ageing process.

All this went through his mind in the few moments when she held the door open and, Linus having identified himself, stood aside to let him enter. She seemed to have a warmer smile than her namesake and Linus suddenly realized it was because this woman had brown eyes. The other's had been light—hazel, he thought. That was a distinct physical difference but how many people would notice it after a twenty-year interval?

'Mrs Ledwell' led him into a small, cottagey sitting-room, clean but shabby. A table under the window was littered with papers and the sofa and chairs covered with stretch-covers imitating chintz. It had the look of a room that was only ever used for visitors, as if it were the only presentable room in the house. Nothing wrong with that, Linus decided. In fact, it was a very sensible policy, especially if people wanting a puppy tended to come on spec. The thing that struck him as odd was the total absence of anything to do with dogs except for a couple of plated trophies on the mantelpiece, Linus cast his mind back to his GP days. Dog-breeders tended to have pictures of their dogs all over the place and models of the breed, as well. If they were successful, there would be rosettes, prize-cards and—invariably—framed Challenge Certificates. Yet there was nothing to tell the visitor to this room that 'Mrs Ledwell' had anything to do with dogs at all. It suggested that either it had never occurred to her that prospective buyers might be impressed by a display of rosettes (he remembered one former client who had covered a whole wall with rosettes she had bought herself) or that she simply didn't care. He wasn't sure which was the stranger explanation. Then he remembered what Ruth Thelwall had said about her not making cross-references to other breeds, as if she had no background in dogs behind her.

'I'll make a pot of tea,' 'Mrs Ledwell' said. 'Then we can have a nice chat while we drink it.'

'You're very kind.' It was an automatic response. When she was gone, he realized that it wasn't only the absence of canine memorabilia that struck him as odd. It was the absence of any. No family photos, no ornaments, no pictures of any kind. It wasn't the absence of ornament that characterizes some rather chi-chi houses; it was the absence of ornament that betokens a temporary stay. Another oddity in the house of someone who had been living there continuously for some ten years.

His hostess returned with a tray. Teacups, not mugs, he noted with approval, but not a matching set. Gingernuts and custard creams were a welcome addition to the cup of tea. All very civilized and it hinted at a leisurely approach to the subject of his visit which could only be to his advantage, since it would enable him to form a better estimate of the sort of person with whom he was dealing.

'What makes you think you want a Truffler?' she asked suddenly, taking him entirely off-guard.

'I don't recall saying that I did,' Linus said cautiously. That was not the sort of question he had anticipated.

'When you rang yesterday, you said you were thinking of buying one,' she pointed out.

Linus smiled. 'My fault. I suppose it must have sounded as if I wanted it for myself. No, it's for someone else.'

'Mrs Ledwell' frowned. 'I don't like the sound of that. Why can't the intending owner come and see them and choose for themselves? Are you a dealer?'

'No, I'm not,' Linus snapped with some asperity. 'As a matter of fact, I'm a vet.'

'If someone suspects that my puppies aren't healthy enough to be bought without a veterinary examination, they'd do better to go elsewhere,' she said frostily.

'It's not like that at all,' Linus assured her. 'My being a vet is pure coincidence. It's my godmother who's interested in having a Truffle Dog. I'm of the opinion that she should look for something smaller and I persuaded her to let me come to see them. If I decide one will be too much for her, I'm afraid I shall lie and say you don't have any available.'

The Other One's hackles became less noticeable. 'I see. Does your godmother know anything about them?'

'Yes, indeed. She used to have them. In fact, you may well have known her. Ilse Trautgarden.'

'Mrs Ledwell' sat very still. 'There's not likely to be two people with that name,' she remarked. 'As I recall, we were very good friends. I'm surprised she didn't say as much.'

'She did.' Linus hastened to correct his slip. 'It's just that it was a long time ago and I wasn't at all sure that your recollection would necessarily tally with hers.'

It was plausible but Linus could see she wasn't happy about it. 'I thought she'd died,' she said.

She did, Linus thought. Aloud he said, 'She was very ill for some time. Went to live with a cousin in Switzerland, but that's such an expensive place to live now and she only has a pension so she came back.' He didn't know whether to admire his invention or deplore the facility with which he lied.

'Mrs Ledwell' smiled and Linus began to appreciate why so many people described her as 'sweet'. It was those brown eyes. They lent a softness to the expression which had nothing whatever to do with the true feeling behind them. 'And is she living with you now, Mr Rintoul? You must be a very paragon of a godson if she is.'

Linus was taken aback to hear her use his name and then he remembered that he had given it to her when he had telephoned. 'No, there's simply no room and in any case she prefers her independence. She has a small flat in North Oxford.'

'A flat? Hardly a suitable home for a dog.'

'Precisely. That's one of the reasons why I'm hoping to dissuade her.'

'Mrs Ledwell' rose to her feet. 'I can save you a lot of bother, then, Mr Rintoul. I simply don't have anything for sale and I don't know when I shall have. Does that suit you?'

Linus was about to say that it did when the door opened and a sullen-faced young man came in. He couldn't have been much older than twenty-two or -three and his boots and overalls indicated that he had been working outside. He gave Linus a more-than-passing glance. 'They've just delivered the tripes,' he said.

Linus instinctively glanced at the window and confirmed his impression that the sitting-room was at the front of the cottage. He hadn't been aware of a vehicle pulling up outside but then, he hadn't been listening for one, either.

'You know what to do with them,' she said. 'This is Mr Rintoul. His godmother is Ilse Trautgarden. Isn't that a coincidence? Mr Rintoul—my son, Patrick.'

Ruth Thelwall was right. It was just about medically feasible for them to be mother and son, but highly improbable. He might be adopted but one thing was quite sure: he didn't look as if he'd inherited any genes from his mother.

'I thought she was dead,' Patrick commented. His accent was more pronounced. Indeed, until he heard it, Linus had barely noticed his hostess's. He smiled.

'Do you live in Lower Shottington, too? he asked.

Patrick looked surprised and glanced across at his mother. 'I live here,' he said.

'A happy arrangement,' Linus told him. 'I'd have expected you to sound Australian, though.' It didn't take another exchange of looks to tell Linus he had over-reached himself: at no time had he or 'Mrs Ledwell' mentioned Australia.

'Fancy you knowing about that,' she said.

Linus hastily retrieved his position. 'My godmother mentioned it. Something to do with your husband's ill-health.'

'Patrick went to relatives,' 'Mrs Ledwell' told him. 'It left me free to look after Ralph. We've been very close since we were reunited,' she added, and went on, 'Of course, you're Irish yourself.'

Linus smiled. 'No, only the name. I believe my great-grandfather was from Donegal or some such place. And now, if you'll forgive me, I really must be going.'

They made no attempt to detain him.

'Remember me to Ilse,' 'Mrs Ledwell' told him. 'Perhaps you could bring her over some time. I'm sure she'd like to chat over old times, not to mention looking at the breed she was so fond of.'

'I'll certainly suggest it,' Linus lied, closing the gate.

He headed towards home until he came to a lay-by where he could pull in and go over the afternoon in his mind. He did not rate it a success. He was no further forward in finding out the reason for a substitute Edith Ledwell, only that, if there had ever been any doubt in his mind that that's what The Other One was, it was dispelled. The fact that two people could have the same name was as undisputed as ever, but there were so many little inconsistencies in addition to the existing formidable list of other coincidences that it was no longer a tenable consideration. It was, for example, stretching credulity too far to expect him to believe that an elderly—in parental terms—mother would go to the other side of the world, to a perfectly civilized country, and leave her son in the hands of relatives.

He also had an inescapable and uncomfortable feeling that the 'Ledwells' had had him at a disadvantage, that they had known something he did not, or more accurately, that they had known something he should have known and didn't, and it was that piece of knowledge that put him at a disadvantage. He tried to pin down when that feeling had first begun to surface. It wasn't easy because underlying the whole visit was his knowledge that it had been arranged under false pretences. When he finally pinned it down, it turned out to have been from the moment he mentioned his purported godmother's name.

Linus cast his mind back to Mrs Warwick. She had mentioned Ilse Trautgarden to 'someone else in the breed', presumably telling them of Mrs Trautgarden's renewed interest and intended visit. Linus had assumed, given the uneasy relationship he had detected, that this would not have been 'Edith Ledwell'. He still thought that, though with less certainty. What hadn't occurred to him, however, was the possibility—indeed, the probability—that that someone had passed on to 'Edith Ledwell' the interesting news that her fellow-fancier was also renewing her interest in the breed. It would have been an entirely reasonable thing for someone to do. Mrs Warwick would hardly have sworn them to secrecy (and human nature being what it was, the secret would have been passed on all the more quickly if she had) and anyone called Edith Ledwell was likely to be interested in the information.

He turned the key and put the car in gear. If 'Edith Ledwell' had heard that Ilse Trautgarden was back on the scene, she would have been very much on her guard against any approach from that quarter. She would certainly be very, very careful about what she said, what information she let slip. The element of surprise having been lost, Linus was obliged to acknowledge that he was unlikely to learn anything new from that source and, since he couldn't think of any other, he seemed to have reached point non plus.

The car nosed out into the flow of traffic and promptly stalled as an unwelcome thought struck the driver. Just when might 'Edith Ledwell' have learnt about Ilse Trautgarden's return? Possibly from him, of course, though he didn't think so and, if not, was it very recently—say, yesterday—or earlier? A honking motorist reminded him where he was and he hastily corrected his stall. Common sense prevailed. He wasn't much smitten with the other Mrs Ledwell but, no matter what her reasons for pretending to be someone else, they couldn't possibly lead to what he was thinking. He speculated on his way home on the desirability of telling Inspector Lacock of the possibility that had just occurred to him. Then he decided that he couldn't face the reaction. The inspector was a courteous man and Linus quite liked him, but he could imagine all too clearly the expression of polite disbelief with which his hypothesis would be received, especially since there wasn't a shred of corroborative evidence. No, he had reached an impasse and, if the truth was told, would be quite happy to let the whole matter drop. It had been stupid to get involved in the first place.

Life very quickly reverted to total normality. Very occasionally, in a quiet moment, a little, niggling, 'what if . . .?' crossed his mind but Linus found he could dismiss it with equanimity and by the end of the week, it had ceased to occur.

It was some time since he had seen his son and a conversation with Trevarrick, his boss, reminded him of this. Trevarrick was bemoaning the agonies of trying to stay sane and reasonable in the face of teenage offspring, expressing the heartfelt opinion that, should they decide to pack their bags and go—now—his only emotion would be of relief. Linus smiled and agreed, knowing as well as Trevarrick that if he were ever faced with that situation, his panic would be as great as the next parent's. It wasn't a serious conversation but it was only in the last year or so that Sean had evinced any wish to renew his relationship with his father, a relationship fractured in fact, if not in law, by his parents' divorce. Re-establishing relations with him had come about by tragic chance and building on that fragile foundation evoked comparisons with eggshells and thin ice. It was very tempting to take the easy way out and let Sean get on with his own life. Linus was determined, however, not to let things lapse and Trevarrick's problems gave him the impetus he needed to pick up the phone and suggest that Sean might like to come out for a meal at the weekend—if he didn't have anything else lined up.

He didn't. His pleasure in the invitation was undisguised. 'You've just about saved my life, Dad. I'm down to my last tin of baked beans—well, almost—and I haven't had a really good nosh since I don't know when. Can we go to Hopcroft's Holt?'

Linus had had something a little more modest in mind

but he said, 'I don't see why not. I'll pick you up about half past seven.'

'No, I'll come round to you,' Sean said, feeling that such paternal generosity required at least token recognition.

Linus hung up the phone with a wry smile. For filial affection, read cupboard love, he thought. Still, on the credit side at least Sean hadn't felt it necessary to dissemble. That was worth something.

Hopcroft's Holt was what used, in the 'thirties, to be called a road-house which stood at a crossroads some miles north of the city. Linus guessed it had always been a pub, perhaps even an old coaching inn, but it had been so much extended and updated that it was difficult to pick out the features by which it could be dated. It catered for good food for middle-management—several cuts above Linus's income group but not in the rarefied stratosphere of haute cuisine. It was easy for someone like Linus, who normally ate a notch or two lower on the culinary scale, to castigate it as gin-and-Jag but he was honest enough to admit that there was more than a whiff of sour grapes in that description. Why on earth Sean should have specified it was beyond him.

The hotel was surrounded by ample car-parking, none of it superfluous on a Saturday night. Even as Linus turned off the road, he noticed that the car behind him had the same destination, though instead of slipping into the adjacent parking space, it headed off round the back of the building. Linus checked the windows, doors and boot as a matter of routine. Even government vets occasionally carry drugs and such checks had become a habit when he was in general practice, never to be dropped.

They had a drink at the bar and Sean explained a little shamefacedly the reasons for his straitened circumstances.

'It's not that I don't *have* the money, Dad. After all, it's only a couple of months since the grants were paid and I did have a job during the long vac.'

Linus murmured something to the effect that that was what he had thought and Sean grinned.

'The point is, Dad, I had quite a job making the grant last out last year and everything goes up all the time. If they put the grant up, then the college puts up the cost to the student. You can't get ahead, try as you will.'

'I don't think that's the idea,' Linus suggested.

'Well, no, but it would be nice if you thought it was worth a try. Anyway, I've bought the books I need for this year and anything left plus what I earned I've put in a building society and I allow myself so much a month. Trouble is, by the end of a month I've run out.'

'Don't you ever cheat?' Linus asked curiously.

'What would be the point? I'd end up with a month's starvation. Doesn't appeal.'

Linus could appreciate that. He was quite agreeably surprised that Sean had tackled the age-old problem of students in such a mature, if unexciting, way. 'Then you'd better fill up this evening,' he told him. 'I'm not undertaking to feed you at regular intervals.'

They were half way through the main course when, with a roar, the windows opposite disintegrated along with part of their supporting wall and the dining-room became a temporary cloud of dust and flying splinters of glass. Linus, as much by instinct as reason, reached across the table and, cupping his hand behind Sean's head, pulled him sideways with him on to the floor between their table and the wall. Now they became aware of the screams of the other diners. After a short interval, Linus emerged warily. One woman was still screaming but the predominant sound was of sobbing, the nervous reaction to shock. The dust was beginning to settle. The glass had already found its targets. He looked down at Sean whose teeth were now audibly chattering.

'You all right?' he asked.

'I think so. I don't know. I can't really think. What was it?'

'An explosion. Probably a gas main.' Even as he made the suggestion, Linus realized that there would be no gas this far from a sizeable town. He looked around. He was not surprised to note that the room was now in darkness and relieved that, as yet, there was no fire. He turned his attention to the gaping hole in the exterior wall. Something in the car park was burning ferociously. Presumably a car. It generated waves of heat which reached into the dining-room and, to his horror, he thought he saw a head rise up in the blazing shell and then fall back again. He closed his eyes. Pray God I'm mistaken, he thought.

Now people were beginning to stumble about, some making for the hole.

'No!' he called out. 'Not that way!' When the heat from the blazing car ignited the ones on either side, they would go up like bombs. Better by far to stay where they were—or to get out in the other direction if there was no debris barring the way. 'Come on, Sean,' he said. 'Let's try this way.'

They weren't the only ones picking their way unsteadily across fallen masonry and overturned furniture and once through the arch and into the room beyond the dining-room found remarkably little damage. Linus had no idea how much time had elapsed since the explosion. It felt like half a lifetime and was probably only a few minutes but from somewhere, a long way off, he could hear sirens. The phones must still be working. Someone had called the emergency services.

In fact, the call had come from the petrol-station opposite the hotel. The cashier's unhesitating testament to an explosion meant that the civil arm was very quickly supplemented by the military. The US base at Upper Heyford was well equipped to deal with fire and once the dreaded word 'bomb' had been mentioned, the base's nearby presence ensured the rapid arrival of the personnel needed to detect any further devices if investigation should prove that there wasn't a more ordinary explanation.

All of this was lost on the victims of the explosion, who were bundled into ambulances with as much speed as their welfare permitted. No one so far was dead but those sitting close to the window had received the full blast of stone and, more insidiously, glass. These were got away first, followed by those who, like the Rintouls, had been either out of the line of the blast or by some lucky fluke had escaped obvious physical damage, the police taking such names and addresses as they could and leaving colleagues at the hospitals to finish that particular task.

Neither Linus nor Sean was suffering from anything more than shock and were dismissed after a brief but thorough check-up. A young constable recorded their particulars and told Linus there would be an ambulance to take them home.

Linus shook his head. 'I've got a car,' he insisted.

'Which you're in no shape to drive, sir,' the young man said politely but firmly. 'Besides, isn't it back at Hopcroft's Holt?'

Linus shook his head again, but this time it was as if he were trying to clear the clouds of confusion. 'Of course. I forgot. How do I get it back?'

'We'll take care of that, sir, don't you fret. Let me have the registration number. Make and colour, too, just to be on the safe side.'

Linus gave him the information.

'Thank you, sir. We'll be taking a statement from you later. Someone'll be round tomorrow, I dare say. What you need is a good night's sleep. You'll feel a lot better in the morning.'

The constable was undoubtedly right but he made Linus feel about five years old—or ninety-five, it was hard to decide.

It was mid-morning when two plain-clothes policemen called. Linus let them in without comment and showed them into the sitting-room. 'Coffee?' he asked.

'Thank you, sir. That would be very welcome,' the older one said. 'Your son still here?'

'In the kitchen. Shall I fetch him?'

'No hurry. We need to take statements from you both and it saves us a bit of walking if he's here with you. You'll appreciate that we'll need to interview you separately.'

'Of course.'

At Linus's suggestion, they spoke to Sean first, and he occupied himself with the washing-up. Uncharacteristically, he hadn't done it as soon as breakfast was over. Neatness and tidiness had no longer seemed important.

His own interview was, he thought afterwards, oddly reminiscent of The Wild Wood—there was nothing to alarm him at first entry.

'Have there been any fatalities?' he asked.

'No, sir, not so far. Three people have been detained in hospital and I gather they'll be there for a few days yet, but they're not critical. Oddly enough, your son asked the same thing.'

'It's been bothering both of us,' Linus said.

'Very natural, in the circumstances. Now, sir, we'd like you to go through the evening carefully, remembering as much as you can, even if it seems unimportant, and starting with why you chose Hopcroft's Holt.'

Linus smiled briefly. 'You'll have to ask Sean that. He wanted to go there. It wouldn't have occurred to me.'

'Not your kind of place?' The officer looked around the room, noting the unobtrusive furniture, the walls whose colour was chosen to set off to advantage the pictures. All originals, as far as he could tell. Not tat, either. Mr Rintoul was not a man who could be conned with the story that anything in oils would appreciate in value. 'I'd have thought it was.'

'Not my price-tag, Detective-Sergeant. I'm a civil servant and I buy pictures. That's too expensive a hobby to allow for much eating out.'

'Nevertheless, you took your son when he asked?'

'I didn't say I could never afford to indulge myself,' Linus pointed out.

'Of course not. Life would be tedious if we always stayed within our means, wouldn't it?'

Linus judged that it was a question not requiring an answer and made none. He wasn't too happy about the tone of the remark, though. He began to feel wary.

'So you don't go there often?' the policeman continued.

'I've never been there before.'

'Who knew you were going?'

'Only Sean—and Hopcroft's Holt, of course: being Saturday night, I booked a table.'

'You didn't mention it around the office? You know: "You'll never guess where we're going tomorrow"—that sort of thing.'

Linus smiled. As a guess it was way off target. 'Not my style, Detective-Sergeant. I don't think I mentioned it to anybody at all.'

The policeman seemed satisfied with that answer and changed his line of questioning. 'Ever suspected someone might be watching you, Mr Rintoul?'

'Not even at my most paranoid.'

'So presumably you don't think anyone's been following you?'

'Good heavens, no. Why should they?'

'Nobody was following you last night, for instance?'

'Not that I'm aware of. A car followed us into the car park, but that's hardly noteworthy on a Saturday evening at a popular restaurant.'

'Did you notice where it parked?'

'Not really.' Linus frowned, trying to remember what it did do. 'I think it went round the back of the building. Why? Is it significant?'

'Everything's significant in a case like this. We're just trying to establish where everyone was. Can you describe it?'

Linus thought. 'The light had almost gone and his headlights were on. A dark colour, but I couldn't say what.'

'Make? Model?'

'No idea. Nothing distinctive, I suppose. I mean, if it had been a Jaguar or a Range-Rover it would have registered and it didn't, and I'm not very car-minded.'

'So you can't remember the registration number?'

'Of course I can't. Would you remember the number of every car that followed you into a car park?' Linus paused and sighed. 'Yes, I expect you would. It's probably an automatic part of your training.'

The policeman permitted himself a smile. 'If it's any consolation, sir, I probably wouldn't, not in similar circumstances, but there are people with photographic memories who can just call up car numbers on demand. You know your own car's registration number, I suppose?'

Linus did, but only because the letters were COW which he had always thought very appropriate for a vet.

The policeman flipped back a few pages in his notebook. 'That's what our records show. Was that the car you were driving last night?'

'Of course it was. It's the only one I've got.'

'Quite, sir, but it might have been in dock and the garage might have lent you another. Or you might have been using your son's car.'

'I take your point. It was my car. Is it so very important?'

For the first time, the younger policeman made a contribution. 'We think so, sir. You see, it was your car they put the bomb under.'

Linus felt the colour drain from his face. He cast his mind back to that glimpse through the hole in the wall. Strange that it had never crossed his mind it might have been his car. It hadn't even registered as being in the same area. He remembered something else, too, and felt sick.

'But there was someone in that car, Detective-Sergeant.'

The policemen exchanged glances. 'How did you know that?' the older one asked.

Linus told him.

'As a matter of fact, we're fairly sure there were two people in the car. This confirms it.'

'I only saw one,' Linus said.

'But from your description he was sitting in the passenger seat. The bomb went off when the ignition was turned on. Between your arrival and then, someone slipped under the car—easily done in a crowded car park—and connected it to the wiring. Not difficult, if you know what you're at.'

'But why should they have then got in the car and turned the key?' Linus was bewildered.

'Who suggested they did? No, we think that was a couple of joy-riders. The garage opposite had seen two young tearaways hanging about. Their cashier's new on the job, or she'd have known to ring the hotel management and warn them. They were trying door-handles. While she was debating whether to go on minding her own business, they got into your car.'

Linus shook his head. 'Not just like that they didn't. I not only locked it, I checked it. Including the boot. I do it automatically. Vets carry drugs and syringes, you know.'

'Your son confirms that you checked. Believe it or not, it's relatively easy for a determined car-thief to break into the average car, and a bit of clever fiddling with the right wires will start the engine—or, in this case, set off the bomb. We'll have a better idea when forensic have had a chance to go over the car thoroughly. I'm assuming you do have your own keys, sir, and hadn't left them in a coat pocket to be picked while you ate?'

Linus fished them out of his pocket and put them on the table. 'There's another set upstairs in the drawer of the bedside cabinet,' he said and the younger policeman, obeying a nod from his superior went upstairs and returned with them.

'If they had a key, I don't know how they got one,' Linus said, 'but it explains how they got in. The same key does both jobs.'

That information was scrupulously recorded. 'We may be able to find out how they happened to have a key when we've found out who they were,' the older policeman said.

'Will there be enough left to identify them?' Linus asked.

'You'd be surprised what forensic can do these days. Besides, sooner or later their mothers may even notice they're missing. That's when we'll begin to make progress. For the time being, the two joy-riders are a side-issue. Tell me, Mr Rintoul, what connections do you have with Ireland?'

Linus stared at him. 'Why should you assume I have any?'

'"Rintoul" is an Irish name.'

'My grandfather was Irish. Not an unusual occurrence, I believe.'

'Quite common, I should think, but perhaps you'd answer my question. What connections do you have with Ireland?'

The inference was clear. Even a five-year-old would have picked it up these days. 'Theologically I'm agnostic and politically I'm an old-fashioned Liberal,' he said. 'I've no views on the Irish problem except that it seems insoluble and, apart from the odd bar-room bigot who says pull the Army out and let the buggers kill each other, I don't think I've ever met anyone whose views are more extreme than my own—and mine can best be summed up by saying something ought to be done, but God knows what.'

The Detective-Sergeant allowed himself another of his rare smiles. 'Not quite the phraseology one might expect from an agnostic,' he commented, 'but I know what you mean. However, with all due respect, Mr Rintoul, that wasn't quite what I asked. I hope we're not being deliberately evasive.'

Linus noted with irritation that he had adopted the use of the first person plural, so beloved of policemen and the medical profession. He was never sure what its use was meant to convey. Its effect was invariably annoyingly patronizing. He gritted his teeth. One was well advised to screen one's irritation from policemen. 'I wasn't aware of any but the most tenuous of connections,' he said.

The policeman appeared to be thinking that one over. 'Fond of Ireland, are we?' he asked.

'I can't speak for you, Officer, but I've never been there in my life,' Linus told him, pedantically accurate. The sarcasm was lost on his interlocutor.

'No sentimental attachment to our roots, then?'

Linus gave up. 'No. None.'

'No reason that they should want to blow you up?'

'None that I can think of. Is that who you think it was?'

'It has all the hallmarks. Can't you think of anything that might connect you with one Irish terrorist organization or another?'

Linus sighed with a mixture of exasperation and exhaustion. 'No,' he said. 'None at all, but I promise you, if something occurs to me, I'll get in touch.'

Whether that really satisfied his visitor or whether he realized Linus's recollections had been fully disinterred,

Linus was unsure. Whatever the reason, the Detective-Sergeant took his leave after advising—it sounded more like warning—Linus that he would be needed at St Aldate's in a day or two to read through a properly drawn up statement and sign it. They would, he added kindly, let themselves out, and Linus was only too happy to let them. Then he went back to bed.

Sean, with the resilience of youth, turned on the television but it wasn't long before he, too, was sound asleep.

CHAPTER 6

When Linus had woken up on the Sunday morning, he had thought that, apart from not feeling entirely refreshed, he had come through the previous night's ordeal remarkably well. He soon realized he had been wrong. The shock hit Sean sooner but he was over it more quickly than his father. The impact on Linus was the greater because it was *his* car, his and no one else's, that was booby-trapped and because those two young joy-riders, however illegal their intentions, should have been him and he felt guilty. It was a complex guilt, in part due to someone else's having lost his life when it should have been him, and in part because he also felt relieved that it hadn't been he who died, and he felt guilty because he felt relieved.

He slept a lot, more than was healthy though he knew if he didn't need it, it wouldn't sweep over him in such waves. It wasn't as if he enjoyed it, either: when he slept, he dreamed, and the recurring image in his dreams was that head. Sometimes it had features, though he had been aware of none. Sometimes they were his features, sometimes Sean's and he wasn't sure which was worse.

The strange phenomenon was that his mind seemed to be running along two entirely unconnected channels. On the one hand, there was the bomb, which was a fact, and the reasons for it, which weren't. On the other was the Edith Ledwell business. Sometimes one occupied his entire mind to the exclusion of everything else and sometimes the other. Never did they intertwine and only a tiny fraction of his attention seemed able to cope with such mundane trivialities as eating. He had no desire to eat and, more significantly, felt no need to. Nor did he have any inclination to think about food and, when Sean prepared a salad for them, Linus picked at the lettuce and tomatoes but found he couldn't face the ham.

He became preoccupied with the question of whether or not the other Edith Ledwell had known that Ilse Trautgarden was back on the scene. It finally dawned on him that this was one question he could settle with no difficulty at all and he rang Mrs Warwick.

'Why, yes, I remember you,' she said. 'I didn't altogether expect to hear from you again.'

'You were kind enough to give me your time,' Linus told her. 'It seemed the least I could do to let you know that my godmother has finally decided against a Truffle Dog.'

'I'm not surprised, though I'd have enjoyed meeting her. If she's ever up this way, do suggest she calls in, won't you?'

Linus assured her he would. 'I think she might be quite interested in contacting some of the Truffle Dog people,' he went on. 'She asked me the other day whether anyone else knew she was still around. I said I thought you'd said you told someone but that you'd not mentioned their name. I don't suppose you remember?'

Mrs Warwick was obviously casting back in her memory. 'Yes, I did mention it to someone soon after you rang, I think. It was at a show in the Midlands, as I recall. I was speaking to Jean Poffley—she's quite a newcomer but very interested in the breed's history. Mind you, quite a lot of people probably heard me—I made no secret of it and I dare say, the dog game being what it is, word went round.'

'I dare say it did,' Linus agreed. 'Was that a show that Mrs—what was her name? Oh yes, Ledwell—that Mrs Ledwell went to?'

'It must have been. She doesn't usually miss any breed classes. Hang on, I'm just reaching for the catalogue.' There was a silence broken only by the rustling of pages. The catalogue had obviously been to hand. 'Yes, here we are.

She had three entered and all of them were placed so they must have been there. Not complimentary entries. Of course, sometimes Patrick takes the dogs for her and I can't remember which of them was there on that occasion.'

'It doesn't matter,' Linus said truthfully. Even if it were the son, to whom the name would presumably mean nothing, he would have been bound to mention it to his mother when he got home. Linus began to make the thank-you-again-before-I-hang-up noises that courtesy requires when she interrupted him.

'There is one other person I told,' Mrs Warwick said. 'Well, not exactly told, because they already knew, but I gave them your godmother's phone number.'

'Who was that? I'll ask her if they've been in touch, though she hasn't mentioned it.'

Mrs Warwick thought. 'I don't actually know. It was a couple of days after the show. A woman, but I didn't know the voice. Said she'd heard Mrs Trautgarden was around and did I have a contact number. She said she bred Salukis and had known her in the old days. I didn't think to ask her name. I gave her the phone number, though. There seemed no reason not to.'

'None at all,' Linus assured her.

When he had hung up, he decided that the phone call that should have cleared everything up had left it all more confused than before. All he had learned was that it had been perfectly possible for The Other One to learn that her old friend was back in the land of the living. And where did that get him? Even if it were she who had phoned Mrs Warwick—and Mrs Warwick had been quite explicit about not recognizing the voice—all she had got was a code and a phone number. Tracing the code was a simple, if tedious, business, involving an index finger and a phone book. The number was a different matter. Linus remembered having once wanted an old friend's address so that he could send him a Christmas card. He'd had the phone number so he'd rung Directory Enquiries who'd been sympathetic but adamant: that information was not available.

He realized sheepishly that he was trying to connect the one Mrs Ledwell with the other's death and without a shred of evidence: no motive and no opportunity. The subject was better dropped or, at least, left to the police.

Linus and Sean duly read over and signed their statements and Sean returned to Balliol. Linus knew he wasn't really ready to go back to work but he reckoned that work, which at least had the merit of occupying the mind, was preferable to sitting around the house and thinking.

A couple of days after his return, the Detective-Sergeant—this time unaccompanied—sought him out in Government Buildings. Linus had still not felt inclined to replace his car. He would have to do so soon or resign his job, which was one for which transport was essential, but for the meantime there was plenty of paperwork around the office.

'Is this a social call?' he asked when the policeman entered.

'I'm not going to arrest you, if that's what you mean,' the man replied. 'Otherwise it's business.'

Linus indicated a chair and asked the secretary to bring them both coffee.

'Have you given any further thought to the Irish connection?' the policeman asked.

'It's been fairly prominent in my mind,' Linus said wryly. 'I still can't come up with one.'

'Neither can we, despite the name.'

'Isn't that a bit like assuming everyone in England called Jones or Evans is in some way connected with firing holiday homes in Wales?' Linus asked.

'Except that Rintoul isn't a particularly common name. Still, I take your point. We've come to the conclusion that the whole thing was a case of mistaken identity. We think one of two things happened. Either they mistook you for someone else, which might have happened if they were going by appearance rather than specific identity, or they simply mistook the car.'

'Sounds a bit haphazard,' Linus commented. 'Are many mistakes like that made?'

'Not many, but they do occur. It bothers us, though. It indicates a lack of professionalism that's very uncharacteristic. That's why I'm here. We're still not a hundred per cent certain it was a mistake and if that's the case, they'll try again, so when you get a new car, make sure you check it out every single time before you get in.'

Linus looked at him curiously. 'How do I do that? I can't imagine you're going to give me my own personal sniffer-dog.'

'Just check underneath that there's nothing there that shouldn't be. If you don't want to get down on your hands and knees, just put a mirror on the end of a broom-handle with a bit of bent wire—a home-made periscope—and look in that.'

'Detective-Sergeant, you're speaking to a man who can just about identify a fan-belt. I know a fair bit about the inner workings of the cow but I'm afraid the anatomy of the internal combustion engine is a source of complete mystery to me.'

The detective was not amused. 'Then I suggest for your own welfare that you learn—and quick,' he said. 'If it's parked outside your own house, it's likely to be something simple, like a package left on the road or in the gutter just underneath, as if it had fallen there by accident. That's because of the risk of a nosey neighbour noticing someone tampering with a car known to be yours. If it's a public car park they can do a more sophisticated job. Even outside this office, how many people would notice a stranger looking under someone's car in this car park?'

'They'd notice, but they'd assume someone was having trouble and it was the mechanic come to sort it out,' Linus said.

'Exactly. They might or might not comment on it, depending on what contact they had with the owner. There'd be a pretty good chance the first you knew about was when you went up in flames like those boys. If I were you, I'd get acquainted with the underside of a car.'

'Have you identified them yet?' Linus asked.

'We think so but there's a few more checks to be done yet. It's not something we want to make snap judgements about.'

The detective's visit spurred Linus into taking the afternoon off in order to buy a new car. His problem was that he needed it then and there or at least, he conceded, by the end of the week, and that meant it would have to be second-hand. Linus did not like buying second-hand cars. He was dependent upon the reliability of his vehicle and, although he didn't know a spark-plug from a gasket, he was scrupulous about having his current vehicle regularly serviced and then traded it in after three years. That way he was least likely to be inconvenienced by something going wrong. No second-hand car could offer quite the same degree of assurance but on this occasion he would have no choice.

He went to his usual garage, in whom he had as much confidence as in any and explained the situation. The bomb blast had made headlines beyond the purely local paper but Linus's name had never been mentioned, nor had there been anything published by which the car could be identified. The salesman was delighted to meet someone who had actually been there and who could therefore reasonably be expected to answer all those hitherto ungratified queries. Linus had never met this particularly voracious kind of ghoulishness before and it made his flesh creep.

'Look,' he said, 'all I've come for is a low-mileage, well-maintained estate. I don't much mind what make or what colour just so long as I can be sure it will give me the very minimum of trouble for the next year or so, at which time I would expect to go back to buying new.'

'One careful lady driver. Is that what you're asking for?' the salesman said, laughing heartily at his own wit.

'Why?' Linus snapped. 'Do you sell those, too?' and had the satisfaction of seeing the salesman nonplussed. Clearly he was the first person ever to make the obvious retort.

The salesman was quick to regain his *savoir faire*. 'Very witty, sir. I wish I'd thought of that. We've a nice estate that ought to suit you down to the ground. Just six months old. We supplied it in the first place and we've serviced it during its short life.'

'Why did they get rid of it so soon?' Linus asked suspiciously. It looked all right, but then second-hand cars always did. It was when you got them home that the trouble started.

'The husband changed his job. Got a company car.'

It sounded feasible and there was no hesitation about letting Linus have a test-drive. He was agreeably surprised. Perhaps it wouldn't be a bad choice. After all, millions of people bought second-hand cars as a matter of course and it was a reputable garage.

The salesman, sensing a kill, ventured to return to the subject that interested him almost as much as his commission. 'So why did they want to blow you up, Mr Rintoul?' he asked.

The question took Linus by surprise: he had thought that subject finished with, so his answer was both milder in tone and more informative than it might otherwise have been.

'The police think they mistook me for someone else. Or they mistook the car.'

'Ah, that's what they tell *you*,' the salesman said. It was a subject on which he was something of an expert, having an impressive video collection of films and documentaries about terrorism. 'They probably thought you were a sleeper and decided to get rid of you before you could do any damage.'

His theory meant nothing to Linus. 'What do you mean, "a sleeper"?' he asked.

'You know—someone who's been planted years and years ago to blend in with the scenery so that one day they can be activated. Given a highly important and destructive mission to carry out without being suspected,' he explained, observing Linus's bemused expression.

'I don't follow,' Linus said. 'Why should they plant this sleeper and then blow him up? Wouldn't that defeat the object?'

'All sorts of reasons,' the salesman said as if the broad canvas would eliminate the need for detail. Linus's face told him it didn't. 'For instance, the sleeper might have defected.'

'From Ireland?' Linus was incredulous. 'The two countries aren't enemies, you know.'

'Republicans and Loyalists are,' the salesman assured him. 'Or it may have been a rival group wanting you out of the way. Or even—' his imagination was boundless when it had the possibility of real terrorism to feed upon—'MI5. If they thought you were a sleeper, they'd want to get you out of the way, wouldn't they?'

'By blowing up a crowded restaurant?' Linus was beginning to become amused by the man's inventiveness.

'Can you think of a better way of convincing the general public it was the IRA or Black September or Hezbollah?'

Linus couldn't, though he did feel obliged to point out that Hopcroft's Holt was a long way from Beirut, an argument that he knew before he uttered it, would be easily set aside. 'In any case,' he said with finality, 'I'm a Government vet and have been for years. I don't think anyone would take me for one of these sleepers.'

'Well, exactly,' the salesman said. 'That's the whole idea.'

Linus gave up but he bought the car.

When he got home with his new purchase, Linus made himself an angled viewing mirror along the lines suggested by the police and practised using it. He still had no idea what the underneath of a car should look like or what everything was but at least he would know if, at some future date, the underside looked different. Initially his amateurish search on every occasion when he needed to use the car was very thorough but there was no denying it was also very irritating to have to allow for that extra time, especially when the autumn rain came pouring down. Inevitably the searches became more perfunctory and might have ceased altogether had he not been reminded by recurrent nightmares of the need to carry them out.

He did nothing more about 'Edith Ledwell' for a long time because it seemed unimportant after the bomb blast. An old lady's concern at finding an impostor in her place had been something worth trying to allay but with the old lady dead and no harm apparently being done by the impostor, it ceased to take priority. It still nagged at him, though. For one thing, the burglar who murdered her was no nearer being caught than he had been on the day it happened. For another, he had the feeling that somewhere along the line he had been given the key to the puzzle and had mislaid it. Perhaps he hadn't recognized it for what it was. Whatever the reason, the puzzle was as mystifying as ever.

Linus didn't like coincidences. More than that, he didn't altogether believe in them. Statistically they must occur but, he suspected, not half as often as people liked to think. He found it very hard to accept that Mrs Ledwell's discovery of her substitute was entirely unconnected with her death, and his own discovery that it was possible the Other One had learned before the burglary that her imposture was likely to be uncovered when Ilse Trautgarden met her, reinforced his cynicism. The Other One would not have suspected that Ilse Trautgarden was the real Edith Ledwell and if the latter's death was not the result of a simple burglary, then it was because she was believed to be Ilse. Only when the papers carried the story would those responsible realize the true situation. Such was Linus's theory and it fitted very neatly together except for two little pieces that he couldn't make fit no matter how much he twisted them around. The Other One almost certainly knew Ilse Trautgarden was back on the scene and might very well have obtained her telephone number, but you can't murder someone down a telephone, and Directory Enquiries won't give you the address. Linus even went to the length of testing whether this still applied. He rang Enquiries and asked them to give him the address for an entirely fictitious number and was told, 'I'm sorry, sir. That facility is not available.'

'Do you mean you're not allowed to give it to me, or you can't?' he asked.

'The facility isn't available,' she repeated.

'Someone must have it,' he insisted. 'Accounts, for example.'

The operator sighed. 'We simply don't have the facility, sir. I wish we did. Especially at Christmas.'

Linus thanked her and hung up. It still applied.

The other little piece that didn't fit was even simpler. He could think of no conceivable reason why such an imposture should be of sufficient importance to justify murder, in so far as anything ever could justify it.

Linus recalled the car salesman and smiled to himself. Given the facts, that young man would undoubtedly be able to come up with an explanation, albeit of the utmost implausibility but Linus was disinclined to put it to the test. There was just one possibility. Linus had never been to a dog show. Maybe if he found out what the whole business was all about, something would slot into place.

He wasn't sure how one found out about dog shows—there was no mention of any in the 'What's On' section of the local paper—but he had an idea the Kennel Club had something to do with their running. The number was easily found and a helpful voice the other end asked whether any show would do, or did he want a general championship show?

'That sounds about right,' Linus said. 'I take it every single breed of dog would be there?'

'Probably. You'd have to go on the right day, though. There's one next week, as a matter of fact. LKA. It's the last one of the year and the last chance people have of qualifying their dogs for Crufts so it always gets a very good entry.'

'LKA?' Linus queried.

'Ladies Kennel Association. It's held at the NEC on Saturday and Sunday. Which breeds were you interested in?'

'Antiguan Truffle Dogs,' Linus told her.

'That's the Working Group. They're on Sunday, along with Utility and Toys—the Non-Sporting breeds, in other words.'

'I don't suppose you know when it begins?' Linus asked.

'In the morning, you mean? Some of the very popular breeds will start early—about nine, but the majority won't start until about ten. That's what's usual, anyway. It will go on until about five but most breeds will have finished by three and people begin to go home then.'

Linus thanked her and rang off. It looked as if Sunday week was taken care of.

The National Exhibition Centre was an hour-and-a-half's drive at a steady speed in an equally steady downpour and by the time Linus arrived, the vast car park was full and overflowing into neighbouring fields. It was going to be a long, wet walk to the Exhibition Centre itself. He fished his green wellies and his Barbour out of the back, jammed a flat cap on his head and turned the collar up before setting out. It was a long trek—he later estimated it to have been the better part of half a mile—and he didn't envy the handful of stragglers he saw either with previously-spotless dogs that were too big to carry or with trolleys loaded down with cages of small dogs bumping over the irregular ground. Dedication beyond the bounds of sanity, he thought. All paths funnelled into a narrow tunnel that led under the railway-line to the immediate area of the exhibition buildings and a small workforce not only cleaned up after those dogs whose owners omitted to do so but also sprayed the ground with disinfectant. It struck him as a useful refinement. When he realized after looking in the catalogue that over fifteen thousand dogs were exhibited in the course of two days, he understood that it was necessity rather than refinement.

The initial impression when he stepped through the door was of absolute confusion and pretty fair pandemonium. Then he realized that there was a very logical lay-out and the confusion only arose because people laden with paraphernalia were still trying to find their benches.

These so-called benches were, in fact, long trestle-tables about two feet high which formed the base of appropriately-proportioned pigeon-holes, their sides and backs of metal, on which the dogs were chained. At least, that seemed to be their purpose, but in many instances it was the owners, their bags, coats and towels, that occupied the benching while their dogs cluttered up the gangways. Elsewhere, the dogs were suitably installed and their owners were ensconced on collapsible chairs of multifarious colours. In some places progress was inhibited by the transformation of the trolleys Linus had previously observed into rubber-topped grooming-tables, some with the metal gibbet and nylon noose which held the dog steady and left the groomer with two free hands. It looked barbaric but Linus's veterinary eye soon detected that there was no risk of strangulation and that the dogs seemed perfectly used to the procedure, though resignation rather than enjoyment seemed to be their mood. The very small dogs were secured in cages within their designated benches, with coats, bags, water-bowls and vacuum-flasks rammed beside them and on the floor between the trestles. Here, too, were the ubiquitous chairs and grooming-tables.

In the middle of the various halls and surrounded by the benching were the square judging rings, almost all of them now occupied by apparently identical dogs, and wherever there was an expanse of floor that was needed for neither rings nor benching, there were trade stands selling all the things one might expect at a dog show, such as collars and leads, brushes and bowls, and quite a lot one wouldn't, such as knitted jumpers with a pattern of various breeds, antiques, and sheepskin gloves and hats.

Once Linus had found his bearings, he stood back for a few minutes and looked around him. He was irresistibly reminded of Hieronymus Bosch's evocative portrayals of Hell. And this was some people's idea of a fun day out! Linus smiled to himself. There was certainly no accounting for people's diverse tastes.

He wandered round aimlessly at first and then, as he gradually realized that the disorder was superficial, overlying a well structured foundation, he marshalled his own meanderings into some sort of order. The fact that he had passed the same trade stand three times when he hadn't wanted to was an added spur. He spent a long time scrutinizing the labels on the varied selection of proprietary medications and dietary supplements on offer at a number of outlets. There were insecticidal shampoos and cosmetic ones. There were flea powders, flea collars and flea sprays. There were internal coat conditioners and external ones. The dog fancy seemed to go for herbal medicines in a big way. There were garlic pills, seaweed pills and raspberry leaf pills as well as a host of lesser known herbal remedies. He was less interested in the grooming equipment except to be amazed a the variety of scissors, clippers, combs and brushes that seemed to be necessary for what he would have thought was the relatively simple task of grooming a dog, and was extremely thankful that Ishmael was smooth-coated and therefore needed nothing more than a rub over with a chamois leather.

Linus might take a rather supercilious view of such a proliferation of variety in essentially functional artefacts but that didn't stop him buying Ishmael a pair of matching, unspillable, stainless steel bowls and later—and after several second thoughts—a broad, black leather, brass-studded collar appropriate to his breed, together with a strong leather lead that had a really sturdy swivel hook, far better than anything he had been able to buy in a pet shop when he took the dog in the first place.

Then he found a seat at a ringside and sat for a while watching the judging. The breed was Pyreneans and Linus's knowledge ended with that identification. His initial impression that they all looked the same was soon modified by the observation that some of them had coloured markings. He tried to watch the proceedings with some degree of intelligence, trying to see what the judge was looking for or at least, how she could tell one from the other. Once he looked with a more concentrated eye, he recognized that there were differences in the substance of bone, in the breadth of skull and the expression. The tail carriage wasn't always similar and when they moved, the pelt on the back of some dogs rolled from side to side. The trouble was, although Linus began to see these differences, he had no way of telling which was correct or which were regarded as the more important features. It was as complex a subject, he decided, as assessing the relative merits of an artist's paintings. He tried learning something from the woman beside him.

'What exactly is the judge looking for in this breed?' he asked.

'I wish I knew,' she answered.

A man behind them butted in. 'I wish the judge knew,' he said, and they both laughed. Linus concluded that they weren't too happy with the judge's decisions.

His interest in the judging of Pyreneans waned soon after that and he left that ring-side and went in search of food which he found in a quite reasonable cafeteria. It was still too early for any serious queue to have developed so Linus was able to choose a table at which to eat his chicken-and-chips and his Black Forest gateau instead of having to hunt for an empty seat. He chose one that gave a view into the exhibition hall.

'Mind if I join you?'

Linus looked up at the man's voice. He did, but he could hardly say so. 'Of course not,' he said instead.

The newcomer was about Linus's own age and looked more like a prosperous farmer than a dog-breeder. 'Didn't I see you watching the Pyreneans just now?' he went on.

'That's right. Couldn't make head or tail of what was going on, though.'

His companion laughed. 'Join the club. God knows what she's doing. She certainly doesn't. Still, that's the name of the game.'

'You sound philosophical about it.'

'No point in being anything else unless you want an early grave. Shan't enter under her again.'

'I take it you haven't won?'

'As a matter of fact I have. My young bitch took Junior, but she shouldn't have. Third, maybe. Even second at a pinch, but she missed the really good one in that class completely. Didn't even place it.' He paused and looked at Linus curiously. 'Have we met before? I can't say I know your face but the voice is familiar.'

'I don't think so,' Linus said doubtfully. 'If we have, it wasn't at a dog show. I've never been to one before. I'm a vet. Linus Rintoul.'

The man slapped the table-top. 'Of course! Not a name one forgets easily. We were at vet school together. John Chilson.'

Linus stared at him. He remembered the name. There had been nothing about the man that struck a chord but now that he had a couple of pegs to hang recognition on, he began to detect familiarities. He was thicker and heavier than Linus recalled—but then, so was Linus. There was something about the eye, in particular, that seemed familiar, and a slight lop-sidedness to the mouth. A mannerism, too, now Linus came to think about. Chilson always had had a habit of fingering his lapel as he spoke. He still did it.

'I can't claim instant recognition,' Linus said, 'but it's dawning gradually. Are you in practice?'

'That's right. Derbyshire. I was an assistant in a practice in Bournemouth to start with. You know the sort of thing: all old ladies with brachycephalic dogs. Got fed up with that and moved to my present practice. Eventually got taken on as a partner and now I'm the senior partner with two more recent additions and a promising young assistant. How about you?'

'Civil servant: government vet. In Oxford.'

'Nice place.'

'Very. I started out in general practice. Quite liked it but my wife didn't. She hated the hours, so I bowed to the inevitable and switched. Then she didn't like the drop in income. She left eventually but by that time I'd got used to the regular hours so I didn't bother going back into general practice.'

'It might be worth giving it a try.'

Linus shook his head. 'I've thought about it from time to time. Being my own boss appeals but not enough to get up off my backside and into the sheer hard slog that building up a practice entails. I'm too old, too set in my ways. Besides, I like my guaranteed time off.'

'You don't look as if you're doing too badly on it,' Chilson said, taking in the cut and quality of the jacket that the Barbour had earlier concealed.

'You'll not hear me complaining,' Linus told him. 'I have to compliment you on your powers of observation, though. I didn't recognize you at all and I'm surprised you recognized me. Quite apart from the effects of age, I didn't have a beard at Cambridge.'

'The beard had me puzzled for a time,' Chilson agreed, 'but I've always had a good memory for a face. I watched you at the ring-side and knew I knew you from somewhere. As I said, it was the voice that finally did it.'

'So you sat here deliberately.' It was more a statement than a question.

'That's right. It niggled me, not being able to place you. Do you mind?'

'No. Why should I? Funny thing, recognition. I wonder how long you'd have to be away from somewhere before you could be sure that when you came back no one would recognize you?'

'Hell of a long time, I should think. It would depend on whether you went back to your old stomping ground or picked a new one.'

'A new one wouldn't produce any problems.'

'I'm not so sure. Look at you, for instance. We haven't seen each other for what . . . twenty, twenty-five years?

. . . You go to your first dog show and bingo! you bump into me. You don't recognize me, but I recognize you. People crop up all over the place.'

Linus looked at him. 'You've obviously been in this game for a few years,' he said. 'How soon would someone be forgotten if they left dogs for some reason?'

'It would depend who they were—and on the breed. The vast majority—thousands and thousands of them—buy a dog, decide to show, and stick it for a couple of years, five if the dog sometimes gets in the cards. If it's fairly regularly successful, they get another one and probably breed. They last maybe ten years, until the financial loss outweighs either the novelty or the fun. More than that, there's a good chance they're permanently hooked. The first category will be forgotten totally in five years—their names won't be remembered—though they'll be in old catalogues—and neither will their faces. If they've bred, they'll be remembered a little longer. More difficult to forget someone who made a significant contribution to the breed and in a popular breed there's an increased likelihood of several people being stayers and therefore remembering people.'

'Take your own breed, for example,' Linus said. 'Pyreneans. What if one of the old timers came back. How many people would recognize them?'

'You ask some odd questions,' Chilson commented. 'OK. Let's take Mme Harper Trois-Fontaines. She's dead, so the idea's academic. I knew her and it must be getting on for twenty years since she died. I'm not sure I'd recognize her even though I'm good at faces, because I only met her a couple of times. Not like you, whom I'd seen day in and day out for five years. As for the other people in the breed, well, they'd know the name. She was something of a legend even while she was still alive, but there are very few people in the breed now who ever met her.'

'But there are some?'

'Apart from me, I can think of two off the top of my head, though neither does much showing these days. Of course, there are plenty in other breeds who must have known her and probably would recognize her, though perhaps not at first sight. If you picked a really rare breed, now, it would be a bit different. Mexican hairless, for instance. I seem to recall there were once two ladies associated with that breed and when they gave up—for whatever reason—that was the end of the breed. They didn't have a high profile in dogs generally and I shouldn't think anyone would recognize them.'

'Not even if they started up in the same breed again?'

Chilson considered the matter. 'That might be different,' he conceded. 'People would connect the name and the breed and *think* they recognized them—and, of course, the fact that they were known in the breed before would give them a huge advantage.'

'How do you mean?'

'They'd be likely to win. Take Mme Harper, for instance. She *was* Pyreneans for years and she wouldn't be seen dead with a bad one. If by some miracle she reappeared, she'd win—especially under judges who weren't too sure of themselves—simply because if she was handling the dog, it was likely to be a good one.'

'Is that allowed?'

'How do you stop it? It's bad judging, but it's human nature.'

'So she'd very soon build up a sound reputation?'

'That's right. What's this all about, Rintoul?'

Linus shrugged. He didn't even know why he'd asked in the first place. He'd only learned what he already knew. Perhaps he had needed confirmation from someone not remotely connected. Perhaps it was just an indication of the extent to which the whole business preyed on his mind.

'I'm not sure I know,' he replied. 'It's a whole new world

to me, this dog game. There was something I heard, that's all. I suppose you could say it roused my curiosity.'

Chilson looked at him askance but didn't press the point and the conversation reverted to the purely veterinary.

When they came out of the cafeteria, they went their separate ways with the promises, customary in such circumstances, of keeping in touch and not letting another twenty years go by before meeting again. The sentiments behind the promises were sincere enough but neither man expected them to be fulfilled.

Linus decided to have a last wander round before going home. He'd have a look at some of the Toy dogs. Not his cup of tea but that didn't mean they wouldn't be interesting. Two main differences struck him. The first was that the average age of the owners was a lot higher. That was reasonable enough: small dogs were physically easier to cope with than large ones. The second was how very much better turned out the handlers were. It might have been a matter of an older generation's different standards or it might have been that older people had more money to spend on such things. Whatever the reason, there was little sign of tatty jeans and sloppy jumpers. Well cut skirts and neat blouses were much more the order of the day and they were accompanied by what his wife used to call 'good' shoes, rather than those awful unflattering trainers. Even when, like their counterparts in the Working breeds, the handlers wore quilted waistcoats, they here had the appearance of garments that were hung up when they were taken off instead of being left in a heap on the floor. On reflection, the different attitude to presenting their dogs was probably a demonstration of the generation gap. Linus suspected that it was probably his own age that inclined him very heavily towards the more groomed effect. It certainly helped show the dogs to advantage.

He turned to make his way towards the exit and realized

as he passed a ring that the Antiguan Truffle Dogs were being shown. He stopped to watch. Perhaps some of Mrs Warwick's information would prove to have sunk in, after all. There were no empty seats round the ring so he stood behind that front row, eventually working his way into a gap from which he had quite a good view. The standard of handling ranged from the almost-professional, where the handler kept one eye on the dog and one on the judge so that the dog was always looking its best when the judge glanced in its direction, to the downright amateur, where the handler chatted to someone outside the ring while the dog, on a loose lead, dozed at his feet. Mrs Warwick was in the class and came into the first category. So did Patrick Ledwell. He came into the jeans-and-bomber-jacket brigade, but he seemed to handle the dog proficiently enough. Linus was able to study him as he had not been able to do before. He didn't form any drastically new opinions about him. If anything, he reinforced the ones he'd formed before. It was very difficult to believe he was 'Edith Ledwell's' natural son. His age was wrong and he couldn't detect the slightest vestige of family resemblance. He still looked sullen and Linus wondered whether the expression ever changed. It would be interesting to see what happened if he won.

He did, and not even the ghost of a smile crossed his face. He maintained his handling stance until the judge had made her notes on the dog and then went over to the side of the ring and exchanged that dog for another. Linus angled his neck enough to see that the first dog was now being held by 'Mrs Ledwell', sitting at the ringside and hitherto unnoticed by Linus. He debated whether to go round and speak to her. There was no reason why he shouldn't: they had parted on perfectly amicable terms. He had a deeply instinctive feeling that he should not, that it would be a mistake and that he would be better advised just to fade away and go home.

Unfortunately, concentrating one's attention on someone, even for a very limited time, tends to alert them to the fact that they are being studied, and this occasion was no exception. 'Mrs Ledwell' glanced up and across at just the precise angle to catch Linus's eye. The natural thing, in the circumstances, would have been to smile, or even to wave: there could be no mistaking the fact that each had seen the other and recognized them. Their eyes had held long enough for both to know that. Instead, she leant forward and tapped her son and when he looked round inquiringly, she said nothing but redirected her gaze towards Linus.

Patrick's eyes followed hers and Linus backed unobtrusively into the crowd of ringsiders but not before he knew the younger man had spotted him. He cursed himself for not having gone sooner and then told himself he was being irrational. He had absolutely no sane grounds for reacting like this and the most likely explanation was that his nerves were still taut after the successive shocks of finding Edith Ledwell's body and them the bomb. The fact that several weeks had elapsed since the Hopcroft's Holt incident was neither here nor there: these things had a delayed effect. Neither argument explained why the other Mrs Ledwell hadn't acknowledged their acquaintance.

He reached the exit with the minimum of delay and half-ran towards the car park.

The connecting tunnel had struck him as narrow, but it was really only narrow in relation to the spaces around it and to the numbers of dogs that had to pass through it. Right now it seemed wide enough because it was empty but that very fact made Linus pause. It was empty and nothing overlooked it. He glanced over his shoulder. A couple of uniformed attendants were chatting by a kiosk and, as he looked around, a van drove past. That was all. He told himself this was ridiculous. The tunnel was short and he would have no difficulty reaching the other end before anyone who might have followed him from the hall had even reached it. He plunged in and ran to the end.

It wasn't much of a run, but Linus was no fitness freak and he was out of breath when he emerged. Alone. No one had entered the tunnel behind him and now that he looked across the railway line, all he could see was the same two uniformed attendants still chatting. Of the van there was no sign.

He made himself take several deep breaths before he carried on. This time he managed to keep his speed down to a brisk walk and only once did he catch himself breaking into a small run. No one could possibly be following him, he told himself. To do so, they would have had to leave their dogs, and breeders didn't do that sort of thing. In any case, Patrick was in the middle of a class and his mother would hardly be able to catch up with Linus, even in his unathletic state.

Finding his car wasn't easy. He remembered that he had left it on the field, not on the hard standing and that cut the search area by about fifty per cent but he hadn't anticipated leaving in a hurry so he hadn't taken any particular note of landmarks that might help him locate it quickly. Then he realized he was looking for a red car with that distinctive COW number plate. It was much easier to locate a silver one with a meaningless XUD.

He looked around him before he put the key in the door. Nothing. No one. Just Linus Rintoul and goodness knew how many cars. He opened the door and slid into the driver's seat, closing and locking the door behind him. He closed his eyes in relief and when he opened them a few moments later the car park was still deserted and he flipped over his keys, looking for the ignition key.

As he reached forward to insert it, his stomach turned over. He hadn't checked. He had already taken the huge risk of opening the doors which could perfectly well have been booby-trapped. He felt sick at the thought and the vision that continued to haunt him, of the featureless head that rose up inside the blazing car, flashed once more across his inner vision. He got out and knelt down beside the vehicle. He didn't carry the mirror on its long handle for the simple reason that he could be blown up getting it out of a locked car. Away from home he had to take it with him or do without. Mostly he did without. He looked long and hard at the underside of his car but could detect nothing unusual. When he stood up, he looked around him once more but he was still alone in a sea of cars. He climbed in.

It took a tremendous effort of will to put the key in the ignition and an even greater one to turn it. The engine hummed into life. It took a moment or two for Linus to register the fact that he was still alive and it wasn't until his breath escaped that he realized he had been holding it.

He fastened his seat-belt and, as an afterthought, locked the door. He smiled to himself. You fool, he thought. You middle-aged, over-imaginative, half-witted fool. How could the car be booby-trapped? No one knew you were coming and no one had time to reach the car between the time you started watching the Truffle Dogs and the time you got here yourself. Not to mention the very minor fact that even the police believe that bomb was in your car by mistake. This business is getting to you. First thing in the morning ring Inspector Lacock and tell him about the second Mrs Ledwell. Such evidence as you have is circumstantial but that doesn't make the suspicions groundless. Maybe he'll dismiss it as daft. What if he does? You'll have done what you can and the police are in a far better position to judge. He put the car into gear and released the handbrake.

Only the attendants saw him leave the car park.

No vehicle followed him home.

CHAPTER 7

The combination of a long day in a crowded and noisy hall, most of it spent on his feet, and the strain of a totally unjustified fear, not to mention the unaccustomed burst of activity, sent Linus early to bed. Ishmael was unmoved by his new bowls, being more interested in their contents than their appearance. Linus scrupulously washed their predecessors and put them neatly away in one of the cupboards, just in case there should be a need for them in the future. He thought the dog looked rather smart in his new collar and toyed with the idea of trying it and the new lead out on a walk round the block, but he really felt too tired, and Ishmael was perfectly happy to accompany him upstairs and take up his accustomed position as draught-excluder just inside the door. Linus read for a bit, until his eyelids began to droop, and then put the light out and snuggled down between the sheets.

Ishmael woke him up. Linus opened his eyes to find the dog standing by the bed as close to Linus's face as he could get, breathing heavily and, at the precise moment that Linus opened his somewhat bleary eyes, Ishmael nudged his face with his cold, wet nose. His tail was waving from side to side. Linus didn't feel as refreshed as he ought and he peered sleepily at the illuminated clock-face beside the bed. One-thirty. It couldn't be. It must be five past six. He peered again. One-thirty. The dog must want to go into the garden. Funny, he'd never needed to before. Perhaps he should have had that walk after all.

He swung his feet over the side of the bed and they fumbled their way into waiting slippers while Linus reached for his dressing-gown and his arms fumbled their way into that.

Then Ishmael growled. It was a low, menacing sound, barely audible but laden with intent. Linus had never heard the dog utter such a sound before. Almost, but not quite, simultaneously, he heard something else. It was downstairs. It was an old house and the floorboards were none too sound. They creaked. Fitted carpets minimized the sound but they didn't eliminate it and Linus subconsciously knew each individual board's voice.

Someone was walking about downstairs. Stealthily. Right now they were in the sitting-room. It might be Sean, who had a key and who would undoubtedly seek not to wake his father up, but Ishmael's reaction told him it wasn't. Ishmael had taken quite a shine to Sean. No one else had any legitimate claim to be in the house and there could only be one reason for an intruder's presence. His pictures. Most people had no idea of their value but they were far more worth stealing than the TV or the hi-fi, if less easily disposed of. They weren't famous enough to be instantly recognized: Linus wasn't in that league, but take them north and dispose of them carefully, one at a time, asking neither too much nor too little, and there was a very good chance someone would get away with it.

Not, however, if Linus had anything to do with it. Common sense told him that the best thing to do if there was a burglar in the house was to go back to bed, pull the bedclothes over one's head and pretend to be asleep until the intruder had left, and if Linus hadn't thought his pictures might be at risk, that is precisely what he might have done. As it was, he tied the sash of his dressing-gown firmly round his middle and picked up the only weapon there was, a rather nice nineteenth-century bronze of a wild boar that he'd inherited from his grandfather.

As he put his hand on the door-knob, the floorboards told him the intruder was now in the hall and as he opened his door, the creak had moved to the stairs.

As soon as the door was open, Ishmael dashed through and was down the stairs and had sunk his teeth deep in the intruder's jean-clad leg before Linus had reached the top of the staircase.

The man yelled and tried to strike the dog with the jemmy he held in his gloved hand but Ishmael was no fool. He was a fighting dog with a well-developed sense of self-preservation and the angle from which the man needed to aim his blow was such that all the power was dissipated before it reached its object.

Linus started down the stairs looking for an opening and brought the marble plinth of his statuette down on the jemmy-wielding hand with all the force he could muster and was gratified to hear the muffled thud as the man let go of his weapon and it fell to the floor.

The intruder was concentrating most of his efforts now on getting rid of Ishmael and was conspicuously unsuccessful. The instinct to sink his teeth in and then hang on through thick and thin was bred in Ishmael's bones. His opponent backed down the stairs, perhaps in the hope that that would place the dog off-balance, but Ishmael was more than capable of dealing with a rudimentary manœuvre like that. Linus followed, picking up the discarded jemmy as he went and using it as a flail. The intruder's head was covered in a stocking, thus distorting the features and rendering them unidentifiable and Linus tried to reach it. If he could pull it off then, even if the man escaped, he could give the police a description of him.

As soon as Linus's intention became clear, the intruder abandoned the attempt to do anything except escape and, as he reached the door, still with Ishmael in tow, Linus noticed that it was open. Whoever the man was, that had been his way in. Let him go, Linus thought. They may never catch him but he's not likely to try again. The man nudged the door open wider and as he did so, Linus called the dog. Ishmael didn't let go, but his attention was diverted and he looked at his master.

The intruder took advantage of the slackening of the dog's concentration to twist his leg out of its grip and before it could be renewed, Linus called the dog once more. The man made the most of the opportunity and was gone, leaving a trail of blood which, Linus noticed with distaste, had already stained the hall carpet.

He examined the front door and concluded that the jemmy had been the intruder's key. The lock was now useless. He closed the door and wedged the jemmy under the panels to keep it shut and only then did he think to switch on the light. He went apprehensively into the sitting-room and nearly fell over the television which had been disconnected and placed by the door into the hall. He switched the sitting-room light on, too. Just behind the television was the hi-fi and in a neat little pile was such silver as he possessed—trivial pieces, for the most part: an ashtray, two small trophies from his rowing days, a family snuff-box. Nothing of any great value. A side-cupboard had been opened and its contents messed about a bit; drawers had been pulled out and had been rifled through. Linus frowned. There was nothing of any significance or value in these places. The value was on the walls. Two or three pictures were skewiff and he automatically crossed over to straighten them: few things offended his eye more than crooked pictures. None was missing.

He went into the kitchen, made himself a cup of coffee which he laced with whisky and took it back into the sitting-room. He sat down on the sofa, cradled the mug between his hands and frowned at the empty fireplace. He ought to call the police but the man had gone. By the time the police got here, he'd be miles away and on the police's own admission on television and in the papers, they didn't give a very high priority to break-ins any longer; householders were expected to make their property burglar-proof, though how one proofed against a burglar with a jemmy, he wasn't sure. In any case, he recalled suddenly, he'd probably destroyed any evidence: he'd picked up the jemmy himself, he'd straightened the pictures, touched the drawers and their contents, and handled the front door. Linus Rintoul's fingerprints would be everywhere in the house anyway, but he had also ensured they were superimposed on everything the burglar had touched. Then he remembered the burglar's gloves. Maybe he hadn't done anything so terrible, after all. He sipped the coffee and looked about him. A television, a hi-fi and some bits of silver. Enough to justify an opportunist break-in, but opportunist burglars surely didn't go around with a jemmy? Yet a serious burglar would want more and there was no sign that anything more was likely to be taken.

The man had been on his way upstairs. Had he expected to find something worth adding to his haul? Had he been aware of the presence of a dog of so notorious a breed as Ishmael's? Few people would knowingly tackle a Pit Bull. If the burglary had been planned, the burglar must have known the house wasn't empty and that the dog slept upstairs.

With that knowledge, it would have made more sense if he had left the first floor strictly out of it and contented himself with such items from the ground-floor rooms as he could expect to get rid of fairly easily. Linus drank some more coffee.

Unless the real reason for the visit was upstairs and the dog was a risk that had to be taken.

Upstairs and in bed.

Linus.

He remembered Edith Ledwell's battered head and he thought of the jemmy. He felt suddenly very cold and the hairs on the nape of his neck rose. He took several gulps of his coffee and was glad he'd put the whisky in it. Think this thing through, he told himself. Don't jump to silly, melodramatic conclusions.

What if the signs of burglary in Norham Road had been 'planted' to disguise the fact that the real purpose of the break-in had been to murder Edith Ledwell? It was an idea that had crossed his mind before but he had never given it serious consideration because so many things didn't tie in, not least the fact that the victim had not publicized her return. If her murder had been planned because she was Edith Ledwell, it had to have something to do with the fact that another Edith Ledwell had taken the place in dogs that the original one had vacated. Right. So who knew she was back in England and taking an interest in Truffle Dogs? No one. She said that no one at Birmingham had recognized her, including The Other One. She had been quite sure the other Mrs Ledwell had taken her for nothing more than yet another casual inquirer. Ilse Trautgarden was another matter. Mrs Warwick knew she was back and knew she was expressing an interest in returning to Truffle Dogs. She hadn't met her but that didn't matter because she had never met either the original Ilse Trautgarden or the real Edith Ledwell. The important thing was that she had mentioned the renewed Trautgarden interest and it was highly probable that that information had found its way back to the impostor who, whatever her reasons for the imposture, would not welcome encountering someone who might know who she wasn't, even if they didn't know who she was. Mrs Warwick did not have the Norham Road address but she had the phone number. However, it was the number of a rented flat. Even Linus didn't know under what name it was listed—had he lost the number, he would have been unable to contact Mrs Ledwell. It certainly wouldn't be under either that name or Trautgarden. Mrs Warwick had passed that number on. There was no reason why she should not have done. If the murderer had requested the number he—or she—had only to trace it and they could pick a convenient time to stage a phoney burglary, presumably under the impression that the victim was the long-dead Ilse Trautgarden. If they could trace it. That was stumbling-block number one.

The local papers naturally reported the death of Edith Ledwell. That must have been quite a shock to her substitute. If she had been behind the murder she must have realized that the real Edith Ledwell had pretended to be Ilse Trautgarden and the only possible reason she should have done such a thing was because she knew someone had adopted her own identity. Hence the letter in the canine press.

If the other Edith Ledwell was involved, then she had originally thought it was Ilse Trautgarden they had got rid of and that meant that, when Linus turned up claiming to be Ilse's godson, she knew perfectly well that his story was totally false. Godsons, however devoted, rarely went round inquiring about dogs for their deceased godparent. Linus was in the phone book. There were just two Rintouls, and the other one had a different initial.

He had finished his coffee by now and his brain was working at a rate of knots. He made some more and increased the lacing.

Maybe the only mistake about the Hopcroft's Holt bomb was that the wrong people started the car. Maybe it *was* intended for him. In that case, he must have been followed, quite probably by the car that entered the car park behind him but parked round the back of the building. They hadn't killed Linus but there was no doubt that the trauma of the whole affair had driven the Edith Ledwell business to the back of his mind and he had made no attempt to do anything about it for weeks. Then he went to LKA and, even more significantly, was seen to be hanging around the Truffle

Dog ring, clearly demonstrating that his interest was still alive.

Linus remembered that feeling of a fear that amounted to panic, and the care he took to look under his car after his initial carelessness. He snorted. Fool! Just about the one thing he could be sure they wouldn't try was another bomb. The police thought the first one was a case of mistaken identity, so they had not pursued inquiries based on Linus. They wouldn't make that mistake twice. No, no one was going to blow him up. Burglaries, on the other hand, were an everyday occurrence and the victims were not infrequently battered to death. The coincidence between his case and poor Edith Ledwell's was not so striking. Apart from stumbling-block number one, it all slotted into place rather neatly, Linus thought.

Except, of course, for stumbling-block number two. Murder, burglary, bombings—these were not petty crimes and they were unlikely to be used to cover up petty crimes. Linus still had not the slightest idea why The Other One had adopted someone else's identity in the first place, let alone why it should be so important to prevent word of it creeping out that such drastic steps had to be taken. That was the linchpin. It wasn't the motive that was important—that was simple: to ensure the secret remained hidden. It was the reason behind the existence of the secret. That was what he needed to know.

Now that he had worked it all out so neatly, apart from the little matter of two stumbling-blocks, either of which was enough to bring the whole edifice tumbling down, Linus had to decide what to do about it. He had three options.

He could do nothing. This had the merit of being simple. It had the disadvantage of obliging him to go through the rest of his life—or, at the very least, the next few years—looking over his shoulder; keeping well away from the edge of railway platforms and double-decker buses; not walking along deserted tow-paths; turning his home into a virtual fortress; becoming paranoid about every car that happened to be travelling the same route and didn't overtake, about every stranger he saw more than once. What was that cynical saying? 'Just because you're paranoid doesn't mean they're not out to get you.' No, thank you. It might be simple but there were aspects that definitely did not appeal.

He could leave it to the police. He could ring them up this very minute and give them his explanation of events. On second thoughts, he would be better advised to insist on speaking to Inspector Lacock. The Inspector knew him well enough to know that if Linus had a theory, it would at least be sincerely held and not the ravings of a lunatic mind. Unfortunately, the police, too, would spot the two stumbling-blocks and Linus could just imagine the immensely respectful courtesy with which they'd point them out to him, assuming he's missed them. At best they'd assume recent traumatic events had combined to overturn his common sense, if not his reason. At worst they'd think he was quite mad and suggest that social services should keep a tactful eye on him. He ought in any event to tell them about this evening's intruder. Linus didn't think it had been a straightforward burglary, but there was always that possibility. The trouble was, the police had so much on their plates these days that straightforward burglaries had a low priority and if he told them his suspicion that the break-in was a cover for something more sinister, they would —reasonably enough—ask him to give his reasons. That would bring him full circle. What's more, if his suspicions were correct, the fact of the police nosing around would leave him open to all sorts of nasty accidents to prevent his appearing in court. Not an appealing prospect.

He could handle it himself. His mother, who had had an irritating habit of talking in maxims, had been irrationally attached to the one that goes, 'If you want something done, do it yourself.' It had variations, principally, 'If you want a thing done *properly* . . .' Its undoubted truth probably accounted for its lasting quality but it did pre-suppose one was qualified to do it oneself. Even his mother would not have cited it as authorizing her to amputate a leg or swim the Channel. Linus had already undertaken, both to himself and to the real Edith Ledwell, to get to the bottom of the whole business. So far he had been singularly unsuccessful. If his suspicions were correct, all there was to show for it was Mrs Ledwell's death and two attempts on his own life but he still had no hint at all of what lay behind it all. So why bother to go on?

He thought about that through the rest of his coffee and then decided there were two reasons. He was basically bloody-minded: he didn't like there being something in which he had become involved and which he didn't understand. And now he was personally involved. If his suspicions were correct, his true involvement had begun with the bomb. He had been perfectly willing to believe that they'd got the wrong car, but if they hadn't, he had a better reason than the police to want to get to the bottom of it all. A bomb and a masked man coming up the stairs with a jemmy were very personal indeed.

Right now he would go to bed. In the morning he would fit new locks and then he'd start by trying to find out who 'Edith Ledwell' really was.

It didn't work out quite like that, partly because he had to go to work. The woman who 'did' for him agreed to come round and 'do' until the locksmith had been, despite the fact that it wasn't her day.

There were some sheep to be looked at in the south of the region and the afternoon was well advanced by the time he got back to the office. He had started on his paperwork when Lisa put her head round the door.

'Your son rang. He said he wants to talk to you about Christmas and would you give him a ring. He says he'll be in his room from about seven and you've got the number.'

Linus grimaced. It meant he had to ring a communal phone and hope that whoever answered it would fetch Sean as a matter of urgency. Linus knew from past experience that students did not necessarily interpret urgency in the same way as their elders and particularly not where telephone bills were concerned. He didn't begrudge a long chat. It was the long wait that never failed to annoy him.

He forgot all about it until he was watching the nine o'clock news when an item on British Telecom jogged his memory. He switched off the television immediately and reached for the phone, knowing that, if he didn't, it would slip his mind again. He timed the wait. Twelve minutes. It could have been worse—frequently had been, as a matter of fact.

Sean came breathless to the phone, an indication that he, at least, had hurried. Linus mellowed a little. 'You wanted me to ring,' he said.

'I was beginning to think you hadn't got my message. I've been trying to ring you at home, Dad. Last night and again at breakfast-time, but there was no answer. I wondered if you'd unplugged it.'

'It was unplugged just now when I rang you, so it can't have been. I haven't heard it ring. We'll try it in a minute. Lisa said it was something to do with Christmas.'

'It's not far off now and I wondered—' Sean hesitated self-consciously—'well, I wondered what you were doing. Whether you'd made any plans.'

'Why?' Linus asked warily.

'Oh, no reason. What I mean is, it doesn't matter if you have but if you haven't, I thought maybe I could come to you for a couple of days. If you'd like me to,' he added hastily.

Linus glowed. It was the first time Sean had suggested they get together at such a time. It was one of those occasions when the thought was worth more than the deed.

'Your mother will be expecting you,' he said.

'No, she won't. I told her months ago I didn't think I'd go to her. She was a bit offended. To tell the truth, she went on about it rather, but then she decided I meant it and she's booked into some hotel where they play silly games and eat.'

'I dare say she'd cancel it if she knew you'd changed your mind.'

'I dare say she would, but I don't want to. I'd rather go to Jessica, if it comes to that and, believe me, those children of hers drive me up the wall. Of course, if it's not convenient, I'll be happy to go to her,' he added in hasty reassurance.

Linus grinned to himself. 'I don't think it need come to that,' he said. 'I haven't been giving Christmas much thought. I don't usually, except to get enough food in to tide me over until the shops open again. It'll be a nice change to make something of it.' He found himself looking around the room, already mentally hanging decorations. A tree in front of the window, perhaps. With lights. Rather grand ones that flashed on and off. 'I think it's a very good idea, Sean, as long as you don't think you'll be bored stiff.'

'Don't worry about that. I'll go to the library and get a pile of books. It'll be quite nice to have a few days of reading something light for a change.'

Linus smiled to himself. So much for Sean's opinion of the engrossing nature of his father's company. 'Sounds like a good idea. I'll look forward to having you. Now, before I hang up, when I do, ring me. If I hear it, I'll let it ring three times and pick it up. You can hang up then and we'll know whatever it was has righted itself. If I don't answer, hang up anyway and I'll ring you just to confirm. OK?'

Linus hung up and waited. Nothing. He dialled Sean's number and his son answered immediately.

'I let it ring four times. It sounded perfectly normal.'

'There was nothing this end at all. Don't worry, I'll report it.'

Before he left for work in the morning, Linus rang Faults and told them that, although his phone sounded perfectly normal to callers, no bells rang at his home.

'Any trouble making outgoing calls?' the operator asked.

'No, none at all.'

'Probably a fault at the exchange. We'll look into it. Your number, sir?'

Linus told him.

'Right you are, sir. We'll get on to it as soon as the engineers get in.'

Linus's spirits were much lighter that day than they had been for weeks and he had no hesitation in attributing this to Sean's suggestion. It was the first time since the divorce that either of his children had expressed a wish to spend Christmas with him, and he preferred not to calculate how many years ago that was. No, that was unfair: Jessica was married and her own family had first claim to her. The first Christmas after her marriage, she had invited Linus to stay with them for the three days, but he had sensed the invitation came more from a sense of duty than desire, so although he was tempted, he had declined. The invitation wasn't pressed and hadn't been repeated, a fact which told him all he wanted to know, even though his relations with his daughter had always been better than those with his son.

He was far more delighted by his son's request than he had dared show and was already making plans to ensure it would be a Christmas to remember, when Lisa came in with the coffee. He looked up as she put the cup down on the desk.

'Sean's spending Christmas with me this year,' he told her.

'That'll be nice for you. I've often thought it must be a bit dreary on your own.'

'I can't make up my mind whether to put up decorations,' he went on.

'Oh, you must! It wouldn't be Christmas without paper-chains and all that. And a tree with lights—the sort that blink—and lots of tinsel,' she added.

'I'd made up my mind to have the tree. It's just that I'm not sure about having things festooned from the ceilings. They always look so untidy.'

'Hmm,' she snorted disapprovingly. 'I've never thought of you as a sort of Scrooge. It's only for twelve days—thirteen, if you count Christmas Eve. What harm does a bit of untidiness do? It's not even as if you'll fall over them, is it? Don't be a killjoy. It's supposed to be a festive season. Who feels festive in a neat, tidy room with just one tastefully decorated tree?'

He rang Balliol and left a message asking Sean to ring him that evening and then, remembering that this might be easier said than done, added the rider that if he couldn't get through, would he be around the phone on his staircase at nine, when his father would call him. Linus had little faith in the operator's assurance that the engineers would get on to his fault straight away, and wondered how long it would be before he could expect his phone to be working properly again. Then he recalled that he hadn't given either his name or his address. The operator had said it sounded as if it were a fault at the exchange. What if it wasn't? He picked up the phone and dialled Faults again. A different voice answered this time.

'I rang this morning to report a fault,' Linus began. 'I gave the number but it's just occurred to me that I didn't give my name or address, which is fine if the problem proves to be at the exchange, but a bit tricky if it isn't.'

'What is your number?'

Linus told him.

'Are you telephoning from there now?'

'No.'

'Hold on, please.' There was a long pause during which Linus felt increasingly irritated. For goodness' sake, he only wanted to leave more details. 'I've just checked, sir, and your phone should be all right now.'

'I see.' Linus was impressed. 'It was at the exchange, then?'

'Apparently not. Something to do with the wires in the street. You weren't the only one having a problem.'

'That was quick work,' Linus said. 'Thank you very much.' He hung up.

He was on his way out of the office before the implication hit him. Directory Enquiries might not be able to identify an address from a number, but the engineers would have to be able to and, now he came to think of it, Accounts probably could, too. His mind shot back to Edith Ledwell. The telephone number she had given as Ilse Trautgarden was perfectly traceable—if one knew a telephone engineer or someone in the accounts department. As that fact registered, Linus knew that somewhere at the back of his mind, if only he could remember it, he held the piece of information that would slot into place and demolish stumbling-block number one.

He went over his meeting with The Other One, trying to recall everything that passed between them. He was sure he had retrieved everything they said but he could find no clues there, so he went over it again and a third time, with no better result. Perhaps Mrs Warwick had dropped the unwitting hint? He went over that conversation, too, and then their telephoned converse, but again he could find nothing significant. It was more difficult to remember everything the real Edith Ledwell had told him, but the information he was seeking must be there somewhere and he rooted around in his memory to find it until he was forced to conclude that, if that was where it was, it was successfully eluding him.

He briefly tried another tack He had previously decided he needed to find out who 'Edith Ledwell' was. Maybe if he worked on that angle, the clue that he kept missing would fall into his hand. How did you find out who someone was? He had already looked at the electoral roll and had found only a false name. The Public Records Office would give him details of births and marriages, but only under the name Edith Ledwell—and that meant the real one, which was no use to him. What about the Passport Office? If The Other One held a passport, it must be in her real name. Or would it? Plenty of people changed their name for one reason or another. Did they risk having a passport in their real name or did they lie? There was one way to find out.

He rang the Passport Office.

'I have a problem,' he told them. 'I don't have a passport and I'm going abroad for the first time this year with the woman I live with. The trouble is, when I left my wife I changed my name completely so that she couldn't trace me. I've been living under another name for years and, although I've got my birth certificate in the bank, the last thing I want is a passport in my real name. Is there any way round this? She's got her heart set on going to Spain and I don't think I can dissuade her again.'

He thought he detected a grin in the voice at the other end and he didn't blame him.

'No problem, sir. You're not the first and I don't suppose you'll be the last. We shall need a copy of the birth certificate, of course, and we'll also need a letter from someone like a doctor, a solicitor or a bank manager to say that you are known by whatever name you've taken and we'll issue you a passport in that name. You can only have passports in one name at a time, though. If you ever want to revert, you'll have to go through the whole rigmarole again and hand in any valid passport in the assumed name. Do you follow?'

Linus assured him that he did and put the phone down, more than a little shocked to discover how easy it would be to assume a new identity. It also meant that The Other One's passport, if she had one and if he could find it—two highly problematical 'ifs'— would almost certainly be in her assumed name. He knew that anyone could get a copy of anyone else's birth certificate for a very small fee. He supposed it might be rendered more difficult by the fact that presumably the real Edith Ledwell also had a British passport and routine checks would have rung alarm bells, but even as his hopes picked up at this thought, they were dashed by the recollection of a friend of his pre-divorce days, a very successful businessman who was always jetting off to do deals in some obscure corner of the globe or another. Because of the time often needed to obtain visas, he had had more than one passport. Three, Linus thought, though the number didn't much matter. A cleverly chosen photo, a careful signature and a good excuse were probably all it would take. And that was assuming The Other One had a passport at all. Lots of people didn't. He was getting nowhere at a very good rate of knots.

Then he had an entirely unexpected phone call. He couldn't place the voice at first, even though it was familiar.

'It's Ruth Thelwall here. Remember? David's wife? He said you wouldn't recognize my voice.'

'Then he's wrong,' Linus told her. 'I recognized the voice, all right. It was putting a name to it that posed problems.'

She laughed, completely unoffended, as he had known she would be. 'If you can remember where we live, would you like to come over for dinner on Saturday?'

'Have you got a spare woman?' Linus asked suspiciously.

'No, but I can dig one up for you, if you want.' She sounded surprised.

'Don't bother,' he assured her hastily. 'It's just that people—women,' he amended punctiliously, 'have a tendency to match-make, selecting the most unsuitable candidates, and I like to be forewarned. I'd like to come anyway, but if there's no spare woman, I'll come with greater pleasure.'

'I'll bear that in mind,' she told him. 'David did try to get you yesterday, but you must have been out.'

'I was in but the phone was on the blink. They've fixed it now.'

'That was quick. You must know someone.' She laughed. 'See you Saturday. Seven-thirty for eight. Will that suit you?'

'I'll look forward to it.' Linus put down the telephone, grinning with broad satisfaction. That elusive little piece had just slipped into place all on its own. Well, not quite on its own. It had had a little nudge from Ruth Thelwall.

In his efforts to trace a connection through his conversations with the false Mrs Ledwell and with Mrs Warwick, he had completely forgotten his chat with the Thelwalls. What was it Ruth had told him? That the young man, Patrick, had been something to do with British Telecom; that he'd been a godsend in the village because if phones went wrong, he saw to it that they were repaired quickly. He didn't think the precise nature of what he had to do with British Telecom had been mentioned, but if he were an engineer, then he would have access to some sort of index that identified addresses from numbers. Then Quod would be very much Demonstrandum and stumbling block number one would have disappeared. It should be easy enough to find out. He looked up the Thelwalls' number.

'Ruth, it's Linus. Sorry to ring you back but there's something I've been meaning to ask you. You remember telling me that Mrs Ledwell's son—Patrick, I think the name was—had something to do with British Telecom?'

'Yes, that's right.' She sounded surprised, as well she might.

'You don't happen to remember exactly what he did, do you?'

'Not exactly. Some sort of engineer, I think.'

'Do you know if he still works there?'

'No idea. It must be three years since I was going out with Bill. This is all very mysterious.'

Linus refused the bait. 'Not really. Thanks, Ruth. I'll see you on Saturday.'

Linus pursed his lips and looked at his watch. It was quite late. If he rang Faults again, there was a good chance the shift would have changed, thus eliminating any likelihood of his voice being recognized. It didn't much matter if it was except that he had no desire to go down in their reckoning as some sort of nutter who pestered them with silly questions. He dialled 151.

'I don't actually have a fault to report,' he told the voice that answered, 'but I'm hoping you can help me. Do you still have an engineer called Patrick Ledwell? I'm not hundred per cent sure about the Ledwell but the Patrick isn't in doubt.'

'I think we've a couple of Patricks,' the man said cautiously. 'Mind if I ask why?'

'Not at all. He and my son were friends some years ago, before my boy went abroad to work. He's back for a few weeks and I'm trying to arrange a little get-together with some of his old friends.'

'We've still got a Patrick Ledwell,' the man said, remaining cautious. 'If you'd like to leave your name and number, I'll pass it on and maybe he'll get in touch with you.'

It was a reasonable suggestion and Linus was annoyed with himself for not having anticipated it. 'That'll be fine,' he said. 'The name's Smyth—a "y" but no "e",' and he went on to pull a number out of the top of his head and attribute it to the Oxford exchange. Then he hung up. The man would probably run it through his computer and find it didn't check out. That didn't matter. Linus had found out what he needed to know and he was reasonably certain —admittedly a certainty based on too much television— that his own call couldn't be traced once he had put the phone down.

Trevarrick came into Linus's office next day. The Divisional Veterinary Officer took advantage of the boss's privilege and helped himself to a chocolate digestive.

'Ever been to Crufts?' he asked.

'No,' Linus replied warily.

'Fancy the idea?'

'Not particularly.'

'You don't seem very curious.'

'I don't need to be. You'll tell me soon enough. If it involves me, you'll have to.'

'It's the Channel Tunnel,' Trevarrick said, apparently by way of clarification.

Linus looked bemused. 'At Crufts? What's the connection?'

'You realize the Tunnel increases the chance of rabies slipping in?'

'I thought everyone did—except the Government who seem to have a touching faith in metal grilles. If they ever got near enough to real life to use the Underground and keep their eyes open, they'd realize that rats just scamper along between the rails.'

'Right. More worryingly, the biologists reckon it will take about ten years before foxes make the trip. They're not impressed by the metal grille theory, either. Adaptable animals, foxes. Ingenious, too. It's going to be much easier for pets to be smuggled in, as well. The Ministry's decided to step up its education campaign.'

Linus nodded. 'Makes sense. Where does Crufts come in?'

'We're going to take a stand of our own this year.'

'Isn't that a case of preaching to the converted? I don't think imported dogs can be registered at the Kennel Club unless their owners can prove they've been through quarantine.'

'It's not them we're targeting. The public go to Crufts in their tens of thousands. More than to any other dog show, apparently. Good place to catch them. One of the London boroughs has been running a small stand dealing with rabies for a few years and they say there's always a lot of interest, even if it's mostly a sort of morbid fascination. We thought we'd up the profile. I said you'd be the perfect choice to man it. You're one of the few Ministry vets with active experience of what it entails. You won't be on your own, of course,' he added hastily.

'Thanks a lot,' Linus said sarcastically. 'Do I have a choice?'

'Not really. I've already put your name forward.'

'I won't pretend to be surprised. When is this?'

'Not for ages yet. After Christmas. February, some time. Lasts for four days.'

'Four days! Including the weekend, I take it?'

'That's right. Of course, you'll need to be there for five: the stand needs to be set up and a supervising mind wouldn't come amiss.'

Linus sighed. 'Won't do me any good to put in for leave for February, I suppose?'

'None at all. Couldn't possibly spare you,' Trevarrick said cheerfully. 'Look on it as a change in routine. The Ministry covers your expenses, of course.'

'If I thought it didn't, I'd arrange to be ill,' Linus told

him. 'Get me the exact dates and I'll write it in the diary.' One day there might be quite interesting. Four would be a bore but with any luck the first would be largely spent imbibing enough liquid refreshment to ease the pain.

CHAPTER 8

Christmas with Sean was an event which for once lived up to Linus's expectations of it and succeeded in driving everything else from his mind. When he finally went to bed at the end of a very traditional day, he fell asleep at once and slept like the proverbial log.

When he woke up some hours later it wasn't the normal gradual return to consciousness. He suddenly sat bolt upright in bed, his eyes wide open, sleep a forgotten world. From a tangled, incoherent dream of teddy-bears and spies, the vestiges of dream-memory plucked the face of a car salesman. A car salesman with a ghoulish interest in bombs. A car salesman who watched too much television. A car salesman who had initiated Linus into yet another meaning to the word 'sleeper'. Linus rather thought there had been one in the film they had watched last night but it had barely registered at the time. In any case, it didn't matter.

A sleeper. Someone planted into society to become part and parcel of its fabric, accepted at face value by everyone who knew him. And then, in ten, twenty, thirty years' time to be 'activated'; to be made use of for some traitorous purpose with a very good chance of getting away with it simply because there was absolutely no means by which the sleeper could be connected with the events in question, short of being caught red-handed.

By adopting the persona of someone previously well-known by reputation but who had not been seen for a long time, a sleeper would not only be the more easily accepted but would also reap the benefit of a long-standing reputation which would make him—or her—appear to have been around much longer than was really the case.

It was risky. There would always be the risk that someone would come along who had known the true owner of the identity, but the more time that passed, the less likely this was to happen and, if it did, the smaller were the chances of recognition—or, rather, non-recognition, of someone's being able to say with certainty, 'That's not so-and-so.' And if they did—well, any organization that was able to research a situation with the necessary thoroughness, that was able to provide the wherewithal to sustain the imposture for years, not to mention the capital outlay involved in setting it up—any such organization would have no scruples and little difficulty in disposing convincingly of minor irritants that entered its well-constructed matrix.

If Linus assumed that the false Edith Ledwell was a sleeper, how well did everything else fit into place?

Very well, seemed to be the answer.

She had adopted the identity of someone with an established reputation but only well-known physically within a fairly limited field and one likely to have a frequently changing population. She had been *in situ* for many years. She had made unchallenged use of her alter ego's kennel affix, she had taken up the same breed, bought the same house. Her only difference at that level lay in the acquisition of a son who was rather younger than might have been expected. When it looked as if a person from the past—from the real Edith Ledwell's past—had turned up, a person who might reasonably be expected to notice inconsistencies in her former friend's appearance, that person had been tracked down and disposed of in circumstances which happened too frequently nowadays to attract undue official attention. Linus now knew that the tracking down would have posed no problem.

It must have been a nasty shock to discover that the victim was not a friend of the person she was impersonating, but that person herself, and the fact that the genuine Edith

Ledwell was in turn pretending to be someone else must certainly have suggested that she knew what was going on. It would be interesting—though purely as a matter of curiosity, since it didn't affect the issue—to know whether 'Edith Ledwell' realized she had actually met and conversed with the woman whose identity she had taken.

Whoever the dead woman had been, the sleeper and her bosses must have thought they were in the clear once more until Linus, in the guise of the godson of a woman by then known to have been an impostor, started poking his nose in. The consequences of that, he preferred not to dwell on. Both stumbling-blocks had been removed. The picture lay before him, smooth and immaculate. He could now take it to Inspector Lacock and not bother about it again himself—ever. He'd have to put up with a certain amount of disbelief to start with, perhaps, but his smooth exposition would soon erase the scepticism. It was a gratifying thought. In the morning—later in the morning, he amended, glancing at his bedside clock—he would give him a ring. Or maybe not. This morning was Boxing Day and it wasn't something that couldn't wait. Tomorrow, then.

Linus punched his pillow a couple of times and then settled down to go back to sleep.

He woke up again about an hour later. A proper waking up, this time, slow and indolent, marred only by an awareness that something wasn't quite right. He lay very still and listened. There were no untoward noises. He wasn't hungry. The dog was in his usual place. Then he realized what it was.

He might have thought he had removed stumbling-block number two. He hadn't. He had merely shifted it along a bit.

If 'Edith Ledwell' was a sleeper, everything else fell into place. It didn't explain *why* she was a sleeper.

Fully awake now and suddenly feeling very hungry, despite his previous conclusion on the subject, he reached for his dressing-gown and went downstairs. He put the kettle on for some coffee and poured himself a large bowl of cornflakes and then, as an afterthought, added some chopped dates, currants and walnut pieces to it. A spoonful of brown sugar and a lot of milk followed and he munched his way through it. When he had finished, he took his coffee through into the sitting-room and groaned at the mess they'd made last night. How he hated to come down to chaos! It served him right for having too much to eat and drink. He cleared a space on the coffee-table for his mug, shoved some papers on to the floor and sat down.

The whole concept of a sleeper pointed to a highly sophisticated organization which might be legitimate, like the CIA or the KGB, or illegitimate, like the IRA or one of the Middle Eastern set-ups. He couldn't quite see why the CIA should need to plant a sleeper in what was ostensibly a friendly country, but you never knew: by all accounts, such organizations made Machiavelli look like William Penn. Lower Shottington was strategically placed for both the US Air Force base at Upper Heyford and the RAF's Brize Norton and it wasn't far from Greenham Common and Fairford. All those sites would be of interest to the KGB and the IRA and when he bore in mind Patrick Ledwell's accent, the latter seemed the more likely. His 'mother', too, had traces of an Irish accent. If the KGB wanted to be particularly subtle, Irish agents—or perhaps more accurately, Irish-sounding agents—would be a sensible move and one which would be less easily available to any Middle Eastern organization, though he was inclined to think the KGB might also have more subtle and less noticeable methods of getting rid of inconveniences than bombs and burglaries. On balance, and on the basis of his total lack of qualifications on which to make an informed judgement, Linus was of the opinion that the Irish connection was the more likely. Either way, 'Edith Ledwell's' true identity was irrelevant, as was that of her alleged son.

More puzzling was why it should have been necessary for her to infiltrate the dog fancy. It was very good cover in that it established her against a firm and politically uncontroversial background. But so would riding, or archery, or the WI, none of which would have required the complexity of finding a breed of dog with a convenient history and then going to considerable trouble not just to buy specimens of the relevant breed, but also to acquire the right address to lend credence to any claim.

Just one other possibility presented itself. When people gave evidence that led to major criminals being captured and convicted, didn't the government sometimes provide them with completely new identities? The American government certainly did and Linus wouldn't be surprised to learn that it happened here, too. That would account equally well for the imposture and would suggest that Patrick, while posing as a son, was really her minder.

The flaw in that theory was the death of Mrs Ledwell and the attempts on his own life. If someone had stumbled on the truth, surely the fugitive would be quietly moved, to re-emerge somewhere else with yet another identity?

Linus chewed that one over for a while without coming to any different conclusion and then returned to his sleeper theory. Perhaps they just planted a sleeper on the off-chance he—or she—would come in useful later. He sipped his coffee and shook his head. That would be a very expensive waste of resources. There had to be a purpose and that purpose must have been already decided before the entire edifice of deception was constructed. In short, it had been constructed to one end, and it was an end that could wait until exactly the right time.

And that, Linus told himself, could be tomorrow—or in twenty years' time.

It began to snow on Boxing Day, the perfect excuse for going nowhere, not even out with the dog. Linus hoped it wouldn't last. He didn't enjoy travelling on country roads when it had been snowing, particularly not to the north and west of his area, where they got very bad indeed. Even the motorway became unsafe, despite the salting that kept it clear. Motorists using it tended to try to make up for time lost negotiating the smaller roads. Very few of them seemed to tackle the problem by setting out earlier.

Sean's objection was different. 'Wouldn't you think it could have started yesterday?' he demanded. 'Or even better, on Christmas Eve. I don't think I've ever had a white Christmas and this year we could so easily have had one if Someone had given it a bit more thought.

'You'd better watch out for thunderbolts if you're going to talk like that,' his father said. 'If I'd known you were so keen on the stuff, I'd have given you a toboggan.'

'If you had, all it would have done was rain.' Sean had no illusions about the climate.

Radio Oxford had interviews with people waiting for the sales to open that very morning. One or two had been waiting outside Selfridges and Debenhams since they closed on Christmas Eve.

'They must be mad,' Linus commented dispassionately.

'It's the spirit that built an empire,' Sean corrected him. 'Don't knock it. You should be glad it's still there. Braving the elements, suffering untold hardship to achieve a longed-for goal, and all that. I thought it was what your generation was brought up on.'

'Yes, and we grew up and gave it all away, and a good thing too, if you ask me.'

Other people were interested in the sales. They detonated

a large bomb in one of the bigger Oxford Street stores at the height of the Boxing Day rush.

The first the Rintouls heard of it was on the six o'clock news. Understandably enough, it was the principal item. Three people were dead and an unspecified number were wounded, some of them critically. Passers-by were also rushed to hospital, having been showered with glass. Both Linus and his son had a better idea than most viewers what it must have been like and could guess what an effort of self-control lay behind the valiant efforts of the less severely injured to answer reporters' questions, unfailingly courteous even in the face of the most insensitive inquiries.

One of the interviewees was a mounted policeman who, together with a colleague, had ridden past the store just seconds before the explosion and Linus was ashamed of his irrational relief that Fate had at least saved the horses from anything worse than shock. Three people dead and others undoubtedly about to follow, and he was concerned for horses! He drew little comfort from the reflection that the bulk of the population probably had a similar response.

There was no speculation about the source of the device. It appeared the IRA had sent the customary warning but there had been far too many people in the store to evacuate them all before it went off.

There was a brief respite from the snow towards the end of the week. What had fallen, melted and while some amateur experts confidently predicted the end of winter, citing an assortment of old saws relating to birds, berries and the duration of sunset, the qualified Cassandras warned that Britain wasn't out of the wood yet and the winter would get worse before it got better. They sounded, Linus thought, just like his mother. In any case, it always did get worse in February.

In fact, it got worse in January, and went on getting worse

until it was well on course for the accolade of being one of the worst winters since records began, a date that was never revealed, Linus noted. Oxford became just a wet, dirty slush-heap. The countryside—if you could reach it and didn't have to work in it—was a visual delight. Ishmael became a puppy again, twisting and turning in the snow, running his nose through it like a small black snowplough and then tossing the little accumulation into the air and failing to catch it. His thin coat didn't seem to feel the cold but Linus made sure he was thoroughly rubbed down when they came in again.

February arrived with no sign of any improvement in the weather. Linus sought out Trevarrick.

'This Crufts business,' he said. 'If this weather goes on, I'm not going to be very happy about driving up to London, you know.'

Trevarrick was unmoved. 'Take the train. They seem to have got themselves sorted out.'

A for effort, E for achievement, Linus thought and decided that a good, solid freeze around the second week wouldn't come amiss. He felt no ill-will towards British Rail but he wouldn't be at all sorry to learn that they were having severe problems with frozen points. Unfortunately, they weren't.

Linus had opted to travel up daily rather than stay in a hotel and put Ishmael into kennels and he was very glad to have made that decision. David Thelwall would have been the one to take the dog in the boarding department attached to his quarantine kennel but it would not have been feasible to get the dog over there. The local authorities were keeping the main roads clear and even some of the 'B' roads but they'd given up all attempts to break through on the minor roads and in the north and west of the county, where the snowfall was at its worst, very few roads were fully passable. It was going to be a long, dreary day for a dog and Linus coaxed a supply of marrow-bones out of the butcher. A knuckle-end and a middle section each day ought to keep Ishmael's teeth out of mischief and his mind occupied.

As Linus had suspected, his presence was not really needed on the Wednesday when the Ministry's stand was being erected by a company whose men knew exactly what they were doing and didn't want civil servants getting under their feet. The finished result looked clean and efficient but neither particularly eye-catching nor very welcoming. Tracy, a laboratory technician from the Rabies Division Headquarters at Tolworth who, like Linus, had drawn the short straw, stated her opinion that what it needed was flowers.

'This is taxpayers' money we're playing with,' he reminded her. 'I wouldn't be surprised if some of them complain about the waste of having the stand at all. Just you hope the coffee-maker keeps going.'

Despite the knowledge that he was superfluous, Linus found plenty to interest him on that first day. The work of getting the huge exhibition hall ready must have begun on the Monday and by the time he got there some regulatory hand had brought it to a state of ordered chaos. It was interesting to watch the chaos recede and the order predominate. Towards the end of the afternoon, standholders began to arrange their wares and Linus realized that the abundance of trade stands at the NEC had been nothing compared to this. The probable monotony of the ensuing days would be considerably relieved by the occasional foray to see what was on offer.

When he got home that night, Ishmael greeted him with his customary enthusiasm and Linus's guilt at having left him for so long was mitigated by the fact that it didn't appear to have done the dog much harm.

Linus went up on the early train next day. It was fast but unpleasantly crowded. He attributed this to the increased use on account of the weather but a fellow passenger disabused him of this idea.

'They've put on another carriage to deal with the increase. It's always like this. You wait till you come home on the five o'clock.'

Since Linus would have to remain at Earl's Court until it closed its doors at half past seven, the five o'clock was a delight that would be denied him, a misfortune on which his travelling companion congratulated him.

When Linus arrived at Earl's Court at what he regarded as an insanely unreasonable hour, he half expected to have the place almost to himself and was surprised to find a succession of coaches already discharging their payload of dogs and exhibitors. He hadn't realized so many people came by coach. They weren't the only exhibitors to arrive early. It seemed as if most of that day's three thousand-odd dogs had already arrived, their owners very sensibly having timed their descent on the capital early enough to beat the rush-hour traffic.

Tracy arrived soon after Linus and helped him check that the video with its gruesome little film was working and arranging their Ministry car stickers and information leaflets neatly on the narrow counter edging their stand. They would be here for the full four days, relieved for a couple of hours at lunch-time by various vets from Tulworth. Their reward would be some generous time in lieu. They were going to be four very long days and Linus reckoned they'd earn it.

To someone who, like Linus, was a newcomer to the dog game, there was a lot to interest and amuse him. The Toy and Utility breeds were represented on this first day, so the overwhelming impression was of ladies of uncertain age, many of them of titanic proportions, pushing and shoving those ubiquitous cage-laden trolleys round and round the hall until they found their benches. Then, the dogs decanted on to the benching, the trolleys were transformed into grooming tables and the serious work began.

Tracy had volunteered for the job.

'Everyone thought I was mad,' she said, 'but I've got a Gordon Setter and I do a bit of showing with him. We've not qualified for Crufts yet, but I'm working on it. I jumped at the chance of coming for all four days at the government's expense.'

'Your colleagues are right,' Linus told her. 'You are mad.' It was not a comment which appeared to upset the girl. Maybe she was used to having her leg pulled. Linus watched the milling throng, still too busy with their dogs to start whiling away the time by visiting the stands. The general public was still thin on the ground. 'Mind if I have a little wander?' he asked her.

'No. Go ahead. There won't be time later.'

Linus didn't attempt to see everything. He was going to be here for four days so he might as well ration his sightseeing. He had a strong suspicion that the novelty would very soon wear off and he'd be glad of something he hadn't seen.

When he came back, he said, 'That Pedigree Petfoods has some pretty slick ideas.'

'They're American, I think.' It was a statement that explained almost anything. 'What struck you in particular?'

'Those hold-alls announcing "Best of Breed" and then the company's name and logo. Just the thing to impress Mrs Jones next door.'

Tracy was genuinely shocked. 'You can't *buy* them!' she exclaimed. 'You have to win them. You have to go Best of Breed at a championship show and then you get an assortment of goodies: dog food and a choice between a brag-bag and a benching towel and then there's usually something else. It was an umbrella one year. They're much esteemed, I can tell you.'

'There seem to be an awful lot of them,' Linus said doubtfully.

'That's only because you've just become aware of them.

Mind you, there are a lot of shows and every breed has a Best of Breed winner so every year the number of bags around is bound to increase.'

'What about prize money?' Linus asked. 'Is it enough to cover the expenses?'

She laughed. 'There isn't any. Well, that's not entirely fair. Some shows still pay it. £3 for a first at championship shows. £1 at Open shows. It doesn't cover the cost of entering, let alone petrol.'

'Then what's the point?'

'It's partly the fun of it. If you want to breed, it's a great help in selling puppies if you can point to some winning adults you've bred. In a way, I suppose showing your dogs is a way of advertising them.'

'So the goodies, as you call them, are very welcome.'

'I've never heard of anyone turning them down.'

Linus learned quite a bit, one way and another, from Tracy. Quite apart from her willingness to answer his questions without ever making him feel they were inane, even though he knew some of them must have appeared so to her, she was able to maintain an unfailingly cheerful demeanour towards the general public. Even some of the dog exhibitors had some rather odd ideas about the Ministry's role. There was a quite widespread conviction that they were connected with the RSPCA, though Linus was unsure which was thought to be part of which. Others had the idea that the Ministry had the power to intervene in disputes with the Kennel Club and one man became quite irate when Linus insisted that there was absolutely nothing he could do to expedite the issue of his registration certificates, and went off muttering under his breath imprecations in which the word 'masons' figured prominently. Linus decided he wasn't cut out for PR work and welcomed the long lunch-break.

This proved less of a change than he had anticipated

because he had to stand for a long time before a table was free and lunch, when it eventually came, was not worth the long wait, and expensive to boot. He was very glad the Ministry would reimburse him for it.

There was still time to spare when he had finished so he had another little wander and this time found the veterinary offices just inside the Pembroke Hall, an annexe where some of the breeds were benched but the press of sightseers was much less. He poked his head round the door on the off-chance of finding someone he knew and was rewarded by the sight of John Chilson deep in *The Times*.

'Well I'll be damned!' Linus said. 'I don't see you for twenty-five years and then you crop up twice in three months.'

Chilson looked up and grinned when he recognized the speaker. 'Come in and sit down. Got the dog-show bug, have you?'

'Good God, no,' Linus told him. 'Purely in the line of duty and they can find someone else to do it next year. I take it you volunteered for this?'

'Always do a stint. Have you eaten?'

Linus pulled a face. 'In a manner of speaking. A long queue, a hefty bill and tomorrow I think I'll go out and find a pub.'

'Don't do that,' Chilson told him. 'Drop in here. I'll see to lunch.'

Linus looked round. There was no sign of anything remotely connected with food. 'That's very kind of you,' he said doubtfully.

'No problem. Kennel Club member. We have our dining-room here. The meal's not as good as it would be at the Club but it's not at all bad. It doesn't cost the earth and there's no hassle. I'll arrange my break to coincide with yours. When do you start?'

Linus told him and thanked him, and returned to his

stand in a more cheerful frame of mind. The prospect of a civilized lunch next day had definitely bucked him up.

Friday was the Working day. That is to say, the day set aside for the judging of those breeds which had originally been bred to perform some kind of work not associated with sport. So far as Linus was concerned, it differed in only two respects from the day before: the actual dogs were different and, as he had observed at his only other visit to a dog show, their handlers were a significantly more rough-and-ready lot.

By and large, the queries they dealt with differed little from those of the previous day. Tracy still retained her enthusiasm, a fact which made Linus feel very old. He became increasingly able to sympathize with the sentiments of that other Sir Walter Raleigh who had once written that he did not love the human race and did not love its silly face. He welcomed his mid-morning break when he treated himself to his second little walkabout, inspecting some of the trade stands he had carefully not visited the day before. He went upstairs on this occasion and was pleased he had because up here were more purveyors of antiques, and assorted arts and crafts. Some were good and some were abysmal but most were over-priced, he presumed because they were specialized rather than because this was London.

He spent a few minutes looking over the balcony. From here he could watch people passing and re-passing the MAFF stand. It was quite interesting to see how many paused by it, how many stopped and how many appeared not even to have seen it and then to compare those observations with what happened at other stands. From here, too, he caught sight of the Antiguan Truffle Dog ring, where judging was in progress. Linus frowned. He had done nothing more about his suspicions nor had he imparted to anyone else that theory he had constructed which might at worst be considered ingenious and at best brilliant. Linus smiled to himself. Such modesty!

He caught sight of 'Mrs Ledwell'. She was handling a dog in the ring, engrossed in what she was doing. Linus drew back. He'd read somewhere that people never look up. Be that as it may, he had no desire to be spotted.

He returned to the stand, glad he had the prospect of a good lunch to look forward to. He hoped Chilson wouldn't have forgotten his offer but one never knew: people were inclined to make big gestures and then forget they had.

Chilson wasn't one of them. He was waiting for Linus and together they walked the entire length of the building to the unobtrusive staircase with its discreet notice indicating that it was for Members and their guests only. At the top of the stairs one of the corps of commissionaires noted Chilson's green tag and admitted them.

Through the door was a world of carpets, space and a lack of haste, very different from the hurly-burly below. The actual furnishings were reminiscent of a works canteen, which rather detracted from the effect, but even so, it was a welcome oasis.

Linus had a gin-and-tonic in the bar before they went through into the dining-area and here he was relieved to note that, although there was a queue, it was both short and good-humoured. Along one side of the dining-room ran a window overlooking the hall below and they chose a table adjacent to this although, as Linus found when he sat down, one would need to be very tall indeed to see out of it from a sitting position. The meal itself was certainly better than he had had the previous day though still unmistakably a result of mass catering. It was the absence of hassle that Linus really appreciated; the feeling that there wasn't a queue of tired, irritable would-be diners waiting for his place. It was what meals were meant to be: leisurely, and he expressed his gratitude to Chilson.

'Glad you like it,' his host said. 'Are you here tomorrow and Sunday? If you are, we can do the same thing again, if you like.' Linus accepted with alacrity.

They were on the coffee when someone came over and murmured in Chilson's ear. He got to his feet.

'No,' he said as Linus rose, too. 'Stay and finish your coffee. No one will chase you out. Take your time. Get some more if you want it. I've got to go—a second opinion, or something. In case I don't see you again today, we'll do the same thing tomorrow.'

Linus thanked him and resumed his seat. When he had finished his coffee, he looked at his watch. Plenty of time. Another coffee wouldn't come amiss. He fetched a second cup but instead of sitting down with it, he stood at the window and surveyed the scene below. Insulated by the glass, it lost much of its immediacy. The sounds were muffled, the amalgam of smells erased. Not unlike a scene from a silent film, he thought. He watched with a general, rather than a particular, interest, the glass barrier giving an almost surreal sense of non-involvement. His focus sharpened as a familiar figure appeared out of the crowds below.

'Mrs Ledwell' emerged from a little knot of people clustered round the Spillers stand. He had the impression that she had not been a part of that cluster but had had to make her way through it.

It wasn't easy to keep her in sight because the ring between Linus and the Spillers stand was one of the two serving German Shepherd Dogs and the spectators around that and the adjacent bitch ring were standing five or six deep, a solid phalanx of bodies which changed its component parts from time to time but never diminished. Only Linus's elevated position enabled him to keep track of her as she made her way between the Collecting Ring and those spectators. She was wearing one of the quilted coats that older exhibitors seemed to favour. Since it was far from cold in a hall so packed with people, Linus could only assume that wearing it was the easiest way of keeping it in sight. He guessed that anything left on the benches would quickly find its way to another good home. Nor was he altogether surprised to notice that she had one of the Pedigree Petfoods brag-bags over her shoulder. It was perhaps rather more noteworthy that it was obviously fairly heavy. Perhaps she had gone Best of Breed and it was full of what Tracy called 'goodies'; it could equally probably be full of samples of the extraordinary variety of dog foods on the market.

Once past the Collecting Ring, 'Mrs Ledwell' disappeared briefly among the German Shepherd benches and then he caught sight of her moving away from him between the side of the Pedigree Petfoods stand and the tiered banks of seating at one end of the Main Ring. A small stand selling Kennel Club publications was placed here but just as he had decided that perhaps that was her destination, she turned behind the Pedigree Petfoods stand and was hidden from view by the structure. He waited for her to emerge but she didn't. His eyes searched the multiplicity of small stands spaced at intervals among the building's supporting pillars but there was no sign of her.

Linus continued to look down on the scene below for several minutes. He calculated afterwards that it might have been as many as ten. However many it was, he then glanced at his watch once more and decided that he really ought to make a move and get back to work. It was a matter of course to cast a last sweeping look at the panorama below and that was when he saw her again.

She was moving more quickly this time; not hurrying, exactly, but as if, having divested herself of the weighty bag, she could walk at a normal speed. She came towards him past the side of the Pedigree Petfoods stand farthest from the one where he had lost sight of her, skirted the German

Shepherd bitch ring and headed towards the Information Centre which stood inside the main Warwick Road entrance. As she approached the wall immediately beneath Linus's window, she passed out of his line of vision. Linus checked his watch again and cursed quietly. He really must shake off this near-obsession with 'Mrs Ledwell'. He was already late.

The afternoon dragged on. Linus found it increasingly difficult to sustain any enthusiasm for what he was doing. He wholeheartedly supported the official stance on rabies but standing around for hours on end answering idiotic questions and watching the morbidly curious cluster round the video was not his idea of a Ministry vet's job.

Only one brief interlude of light relief and that was when the PA system, which had previously confined itself to calls for judges or stewards to report to the Crufts office, and similar excitements, announced—after demanding the attention of all members of staff—'A judge has mislaid his bowler hat and is very concerned.' This piece of information was then repeated. It was a totally unimportant message but it appealed to Linus's sense of humour. He hadn't known judges wore bowler hats. Most of them seemed to be women, anyway. Perhaps this one was some sort of VIP. To have so trivial an item announced in such a way suggested either an inflated sense of importance or a very strange sense of humour.

Linus thought it might be amusing to meet the gentleman concerned. Then he dismissed the speculation from his mind to deal with a dear old lady who insisted upon telling him how sad it was that the expense of quarantine made it impossible for tourists to rescue some of the thousands of cats that haunted the Colosseum in Rome. Like many people, she thought the fees went straight into the government's coffers and when he assured her that quarantine establishments were privately run, she shook her head.

'I think you will find you are mistaken, young man. Clem Attlee would never have allowed it.'

There was no point in arguing with her so he said, with perfect truth, that he had forgotten to take the late Mr Attlee into account and they parted on excellent terms. When she had gone, he turned to Tracy.

'I'm sorry,' he said, 'but I can't take much more of this. D'you mind if I take a break?'

'Go ahead. I'll have one when you get back, if that's all right with you.'

Linus assured her it was and headed towards the Warwick Road entrance where there was a reasonably secluded bar. For some reason the escalator had been stopped, he noticed. Very irritating for people who found stairs difficult. He cut through between the German Shepherd rings and behind the Kennel Club stand. As he passed the main entrance he noticed that the concourse outside the glass doors was empty of any people other than commissionaires. He looked at his watch. It was just after three o'clock. Surely the supply of visitors hadn't dried up as early as this? He tried to remember what it had been like the previous day but it wasn't the sort of thing one took notice of except when it thrust itself forward. He looked out more searchingly, past the commissionaires and past the main outer doors. Not only was there no one there, but there was no traffic passing the iron railings outside. He turned to the man in the brown uniform of an Earl's Court employee.

'What's happened? The street looks empty. What's going on?'

The man shrugged. 'Don't ask me, mate. We're the last to know. I did hear something about a burst water-main and they've closed the street to make everyone use the diversion they've set up. Won't be long before the Friday rush-hour,' he added by way of further explanation. 'It's only rumour, mind. Me, I just do as I'm told.'

Linus saw nothing to cavil at in this explanation but he changed direction. Maybe a cup of tea would be more welcome than a drink. A small altercation caught his attention. A few feet from the end of the Newfoundland benches, a man and woman were in obvious dispute. Their voices were lowered but their gestures were those of two people who no longer need to pretend. Husband and wife, Linus deduced. The husband was the more anxious and his gestures repeatedly indicated the exit that led to the outside exercise area. Linus unashamedly stretched his ears.

'No, now,' the man insisted. 'Just grab the dog and take him outside. Let him spend and then *run*,'

'You know perfectly well we can't go till after six o'clock. It isn't even close enough to pretend your watch is wrong. You go if you want. I'll find my own way home, if watching the snooker is that important to you.'

'I'm telling you, there's something up and we'd be better off out of it. We'll get away with it if you leave all the baggage behind.'

'You know what's wrong with you, don't you? You've been in the bar too long, that's what. If you think I'm going to risk a Rule 17 hearing, you can think again.'

The husband didn't look to Linus like a man who had been in the bar too long, though sometimes it was hard to tell. He left the little scene and went over to the exit doors that gave on to the sawdust-covered exercise area roped off outside. Whatever was bothering the man was out there. It only needed a slight push to open the door and the first thing that struck Linus when he emerged was that the exercise area was empty.

The second thing he noticed was the number of people outside. Soldiers, mostly, and the occasional policeman. To his right the projection of the West Brompton entrance cut off a view of anything that lay beyond it which included, Linus knew, an extensive car park. To his left, where the forecourt widened, he could see a fire engine and its attendants.

He took in all this in the few seconds before a member of the Earl's Court staff detached himself from a small knot of policemen and came over.

'Sorry, sir. This exit is for dogs only. If you wouldn't mind going back inside.'

'What's going on?' It was a natural question.

'Nothing to worry about, sir. Burst water-main, I believe.'

'And that needs the army?'

'So they seem to think, sir. I just do as I'm told.'

'Earl's Court is very fortunate in its staff,' Linus said sardonically, but he went back into the hall.

The husband had been right. Something was definitely up. Linus looked about him. It was difficult for a man of only moderate height to see a great deal in a crowded exhibition hall, but three things became clear. People were being allowed to come down the escalators and stairs, but not to go up; the public was being allowed out of the Philbeach entrance but not, as far as Linus could make out, exhibitors; there were an awful lot of brown Earl's Court uniforms about. What's more, there was a purposefulness about their stance and their movements that had been lacking before. A burst water-main in the street outside might—just might—account for the presence of the military in addition to the other, civil, organizations who certainly would need to be called in but Linus could think of no reason why it should result in any change in procedure inside the building.

On the other hand, there was one thing that would account for both occurrences.

Then why didn't they evacuate the building immediately? There were plenty of doors. Linus had no idea how long it would take them to get this number of people out, but if they threw them all open and made an announcement, it couldn't be long, even allowing for the confusion the inevitable panic would cause. It was the dogs that would make it difficult. How many exhibitors would be willing to leave their dogs? No. Get the public out first (and he had already observed that they were being allowed to leave) and then deal with the exhibitors.

He hurried back to the MAFF stand. Tracy picked up her handbag when she saw him.

'I'm going to find a cup of tea,' she told him.

Linus led her to one side and lowered his voice. 'Don't do that,' he told her. 'Make your way over to the Philbeach entrance and go out as if you were an ordinary member of the public. Then go home.'

She stared at him. 'What on earth for? That would leave you here on your own until half past seven. Besides, I want to see what wins the Group.'

'Look, it's quite likely I'm paranoid and it's even more likely I'm just wrong, but I've a funny feeling something's up. If I'm right, then you need to get out before everyone else realizes things aren't as they should be.'

'Then why don't you come with me?'

'Because someone ought to be here if I *am* wrong, and I'm the more senior.'

She studied his face for a moment. 'You're dead serious, aren't you?' she said.

Linus winced. 'I wish you'd phrased that differently but, yes, I'm serious.'

She slipped her coat on. 'All right,' she said. 'I'll have my cup of tea up the street somewhere but I'm not going home and I may very well come back when I've thought it over.'

'You do that,' Linus said, knowing that if he proved right, she wouldn't be allowed back, even if nothing untoward had happened.

As she disappeared through the crowds. Linus gripped

the edge of the narrow counter, gulped hard and took several deep breaths. One bomb in a lifetime was enough for anyone. He didn't give a damn about the MAFF stand and once he was sure Tracy had gone, he rather thought he'd follow her. He had sent her packing first because she was the conscientious sort who wouldn't have thought it right for them both to walk out and leave the stand unattended. He took several more deep breaths to stem the rising panic and closed his eyes to facilitate the exercise. Then he opened them suddenly and stood very still, not breathing, not blinking.

An image flashed across his retina, as clear as if it were happening now.

No. Two images.

'Mrs Ledwell' with a heavy brag-bag. 'Mrs Ledwell' returning without it and heading, not for her benches, but for the main entrance.

Linus had fewer compunctions about leaving the stand unattended than would have assailed Tracy. He went as quickly as he could to the Truffle Dog benches. There was no sign of her.

'Is Mrs Ledwell about?' he asked the first person he saw.

'No. She went off somewhere. Those are her dogs.' The woman nodded down the benches, to where a flurry of prize-cards indicated Mrs Ledwell's success. 'She's been gone some time, actually. She shouldn't be long.'

'Is Patrick around?'

'He was, but he went off, too. I expect they went for a late lunch.'

Linus didn't bother to thank her and he was quite sure there was no point in waiting for her. He grabbed the first Earl's Court uniform he came across.

'Are you security?' he asked. 'Or just a commissionaire?'

The man detached himself from Linus's hand. 'Right now I'm security. Why? What've you lost?'

'Nothing. Take me to your superior.'

The young man opened his mouth as if he were going to say something, thought better of it and said instead, 'Come with me.'

He interpreted Linus's instruction quite literally and handed him over to an older man who was quite clearly only one step further up in the hierarchy.

'For God's sake,' Linus said impatiently. 'If you're looking for a bomb, I think I know what it should look like and roughly where it is.'

A message murmured into his radio brought two policemen, one of them with a lot of silver braid, on the scene in flatteringly speedy time.

'I think you're looking for one of those Best of Breed brag-bags and I think it will be somewhere near the grandstand behind the Pedigree Petfoods stand.'

The younger of the two policemen passed this message on and the more senior led Linus away and handed him over to colleagues in plain clothes. 'This is the gentleman who has information about a bomb,' he said.

'I see,' one of them said. 'And you are . . .?'

Linus gave them his name and address, his occupation and his reason for being at Crufts. He also told them about his involvement in the Hopcroft's Holt bombing. One of the plain-clothes men slipped quietly away at that and Linus suspected that he had gone to confirm with Thames Valley that this was so. His suspicion was justified when the man returned shortly and nodded to his colleagues. There was a perceptible easing of the tension in the room, as if the police had decided they weren't dealing with a madman on the one hand or an over-confident terrorist on the other but Linus's explanation of exactly why he suspected 'Edith Ledwell' sounded far-fetched even to his ears and his reason for not conveying his suspicions to the proper authorities had an even weaker ring to it.

One of the radios buzzed and its owner listened briefly and then interrupted Linus's questioning.

'They've found it. Mr Rintoul was right.'

'Now what?' Linus asked.

'Now we clear the hall—fast. The public's mostly gone, we've been quietly easing them out. Now we tackle the exhibitors.'

'May I go, too?' Linus asked. 'Frankly, one bombing is enough for me. You've checked me out. You know where to find me. I should think tomorrow will do to make a statement.'

'Thames Valley seem to think you're straight enough, if eccentric, and we're going to have our work cut out for a bit. Yes, we can let you go. Don't bother with the Underground. Nothing's stopping at Earl's Court or West Brompton.'

Linus thanked them and retrieved the driving licence and his MAFF ID which the police had required to see.

As he made his way towards the Philbeach entrance, a message rang out over the PA system. Once more it called all staff. Then followed the message: 'The judge's bowler has been found.' Linus grinned to himself. He should have guessed—a pre-arranged code. It was obviously not only the code by which staff would know the bomb had been identified but also told them what to do next, for the brown uniforms were moving towards the exit doors that formed a sizeable proportion of the exterior walls of the building. If these were thrown open, the exhibitors and remaining members of the public would be able to get out very quickly. Linus wasn't so sure about their dogs.

On a sudden impulse he changed direction and headed back rapidly towards the Truffle Dogs. Another announcement accompanied him requesting all exhibitors to return to their benches. Good, Linus thought. That meant people were going to be allowed to take their dogs out. Since it was reasonable to assume that both 'Mrs Ledwell' and Patrick were long gone, he would see to her dogs.

All dogs were secured to their benches by chains. Linus searched briefly for leads but could find none. He would just have to walk them out on the cumbersome benching chains so, with that in mind, he unfastened first one and then the other of the two dogs. The first dog jumped off his bench and shook himself, delighted to be able to stretch but as soon as the adjacent exhibitors saw a stranger unfastening the dogs, they surrounded him.

'What do you think you're at?' 'You can't do that!' 'Those aren't your dogs!' These were some of the more polite expressions of concern.

'It's not the way it looks,' Linus said. 'You see . . .'

Before he could begin an explanation which, though true, would most certainly be disbelieved, there was another announcement and as it commenced, a chill wind blew through the hall as all the exit doors were simultaneously opened.

'Attention all exhibitors. Attention all exhibitors. A bomb has been located in the building. A bomb has been located in the building. Please proceed to the nearest exit. Please proceed to the nearest exit. Do not take your dogs. Repeat: do not take your dogs.'

There was a brief, stunned silence during which people simply stared at each other and then pandemonium broke loose.

'If they think I'm leaving my dogs, they've got another think coming,' a woman close to Linus said.

'If my dogs go up, I go with them,' he heard someone else promise and, as the dogs sensed the rising panic of their owners, their own crescendo of barks was added to the general uproar.

Linus had both dogs off their benches now and he hesitated briefly. It made sense to give the priority of escape to people rather than dogs, but his job was the welfare of animals and if he could save just two of them, then he would. His attention was drawn by a localized hullaballoo from above and he glanced up in its direction. The security staff were not letting people use the escalators even though they had been stopped, and those that were being turned back were colliding with those behind who were pressing forward in ignorance of the situation. A recipe for disaster, Linus thought.

'Come on, dogs,' he said. 'Let's go.'

Some exhibitors had obeyed their instructions, particularly those with big, strong, aggressive breeds. Others were struggling to control their dogs in the general mêlée which by now was further complicated by the fact that priority through the doors was being given to those who had left their dogs behind.

Some exhibitors, their common sense having apparently deserted them, were frantically collecting together all the paraphernalia they had brought with them, determined to leave nothing behind. He heard one woman muttering under her breath about 'bloody looters'. Not, he would have thought, a matter of major concern in the circumstances.

A few of the smaller breeds had been brought in trolley-borne cages and he was amazed to see a couple of Corgi-owners desperately fastening dog-filled cages on to their trolleys, oblivious of the fact that it would have been simpler and quicker to take the dogs on their leads. It made him wonder what sort of chaos would have ensued had this alert happened the day before, when almost half the dogs had been similarly transported.

It wasn't easy to push his way with two strange dogs on unwieldy benching chains through a jostling horde of sobbing women and shouting men whose own dogs were diving this way and that, tangling leads round legs, terrified by the lack of discipline they sensed and the pervading mood of fear. A scream from above halted Linus and some others and they looked up and back in time to see one of the stalwarts in brown disappear under the canopy of the escalator as the crowd he had been holding back surged down the steps.

'Poor sod,' said a man's voice at Linus's elbow before putting his own survival to the fore and shoving past him.

The blast when it came was mind-shatteringly loud. Confined as it was by the concrete walls, it had no opportunity of dissipating in the open air and Linus, as he was blown forward and off his feet by the blast, felt as if his head itself was exploding. His hands went instinctively to his ears and the dogs bolted. Linus scarcely noticed. When he brought his hand away, there was blood on it and he couldn't move his legs. They felt as if a heavy weight was holding them down but they didn't hurt. Oh my God! he thought. That's it. I'm paralysed. Then he looked over his shoulder. A very large woman had fallen over his legs and now lay there, unmoving. Linus forced his legs to move, to pull themselves out from under her. He didn't know whether she was dead or merely unconscious and he was in no state to ascertain which. He had a shrewd idea, however, that she had inadvertently shielded him from much of the blast.

So loud had the explosion been that it had seemed to be followed by deep silence and perhaps it was for a few seconds. By the time Linus was able to take notice of anything, any such silence had been a mere hiatus, for the air was now full of groans and sobs though not yet rent with the screams of severely wounded as the rescue services moved them. Dogs still chained to their benches whimpered and yelped, while those that, like the two Truffle Dogs, could bolt had done so.

There was fire, too. Linus had sensed, rather than seen, the sheet of flame that had gone up behind him almost simultaneously with the explosion and now trade stands, composed largely of wood and hardboard, were burning solidly. It was as if the bomb had been deliberately sited to cause alarm among the exhibitors rather than extensive damage to the exhibits—certainly the building itself seemed little harmed and if the fire could be kept away from the wooden bases of the benching, perhaps most of the dogs could be saved. Linus struggled to his feet. He was a vet. He must do something.

'Come on, mate, outside,' a voice beside him said. He looked round. A fireman put his arm round Linus's shoulder and led him towards an exit that no longer had any doors to close. 'They'll see you all right,' he went on, handing him over to an ambulanceman. 'Take you to hospital until you're ready to go home.'

'No,' Linus said. 'Not now. Not yet. I'm all right. A bit shaken, that's all. I've got to get back inside. I'm a vet, you see. There's all those dogs in there. We've got to get them out.'

The fireman had gone. 'You can be a vet to your heart's content later on,' the ambulance-driver told him. 'They'll do what they can, you can be sure of that. Right now they'll want to check you out.' He put a blanket round Linus's shoulders with as much care as if Linus had been some frail old lady and led him round to the back of the building. He handed him over to a nurse. 'Just shock, I think,' he said, and was gone.

This was where the bulk of the emergency services were congregated, their work hampered by the rows of exhibitors' cars, many of which had been manhandled out of the way to make room for the ambulances that were now leaving in convoys. Milling about between the cars were those exhibitors, not sufficiently injured to warrant increasing the burden on over-stretched hospitals, but unable to get their cars out of the car park and unfit to drive them if they did.

The WVS was dispensing hot, sweet tea from a mobile

café and the nurse brought Linus a polystyrene cup of it to drink while she waited for the doctor to confirm that he was uninjured beyond a few grazes incurred when he hit the ground.

'Where are you from?' she asked.

'Oxford,' Linus told her.

'Did you drive here?'

'No. I came on the train. One of the Intercity ones,' he added irrelevantly.

'Good. That makes it easier. If the doctor releases you, and I expect he will, we'll put you in a taxi and they'll see you get safely to the station. When you get home, go to bed and stay there for as long as it takes.' She hesitated. 'Was your wife with you today?'

'No wife,' Linus told her. 'I live alone.'

'Fine. Then get a neighbour to look in on you from time to time.'

Linus sipped his tea while he waited for the doctor and pondered the incongruity of the tall, concave-sided triangle that was the Empress State Building. It offended his eye. This might not be one of the more beautiful parts of London, but that shouldn't mean any architectural horror went. A man was kicking up a fuss about something. Linus tried to focus his attention on him. It proved very difficult, but he had the feeling that if he didn't make the effort, he might lose grip of himself.

The doctor arrived just then and Linus had to switch his entire attention to him. The doctor confirmed the nurse's opinion but was less happy about letting Linus find his way home.

'Is there a relative we can contact to come and fetch you?' he asked.

'I've a son, but it's not always easy to get hold of him,' Linus said. 'I'll be all right. The nurse said something about getting me a taxi.' He felt in his pocket and brought out some small change. 'I can probably manage it. I thought I had more than that.'

'You won't need it this end,' the doctor told him. 'The cabbies are ferrying genuine victims of this little lot anywhere within the London area for free. Their gesture of help. You'll need to take one the other end, though. Any problem there?'

'None at all,' Linus told him. 'I'll have some more tea before I go.'

'Take your time,' the doctor said. 'If you stay near the tea-wagon, the cabbies will pick you up there. You won't be the only one waiting.'

Linus, still clutching the blanket round him, went across to the tea-wagon. Someone had found some seats from somewhere and when he had collected another polystyrene cup of tea he sank down gratefully on one of them.

He was half way through it when a sequence of rapid-fire cracks like pistol shots rang out. They were followed by silence and then, in a cloud of dust and a roar like the end of the world, the tall, concave-sided finger of the Empress State Building collapsed in on itself.

CHAPTER 9

'There goes dinner,' Linus heard a soldier say. Then the impact of the blast hit the tea-wagon and sent it crashing on to its face several yards away and there it splintered into unrecognizable debris among the screams of the women inside. Simultaneously, its gas cylinders exploded, setting fire to any adjacent debris and, inevitably, several cars.

Linus and one or two others had been protected from the actual blast by the bulk of the tea-wagon but only the instinct to run saved any of them from its debris. Instinct was little help in the ensuing succession of exploding petrol-tanks and the intolerable wave of heat they generated. There was no sign of help. The second, and unexpected, blast seemed to have completely disorientated the rescue services which were already on the site to deal with the consequences of the first, anticipated, explosion. No one came to help Linus or any of the other wounded and dying now spreadeagled across the tarmac or over the bonnets of cars. Linus was among the former and he pulled himself tentatively to a sitting position, shielding his face from the heat as more cars exploded into flames as the temperature around them rose. The fires were mainly ahead of him and to one side, among the remains of the skyscraper. The exit from the car park to the street was strewn with rubble and the remains of the ticket kiosk but there was no fire in that direction.

Linus struggled to his feet and stood unsteadily for a few moments before picking his way shakily over the bricks and concrete towards the street. He had no recollection of which way he turned nor of how far he stumbled along, his feet crunching over the broken glass from the thousands of windows shattered in the blast before he saw a taxi but when he did, he remembered what he had been told, and hailed it.

'Paddington,' he said when it stopped.

The driver shook his head. 'No, mate. You needs an 'ospital.'

'I'm OK,' Linus told him and clambered with difficulty into the back. 'The doctor went over me. He says I'm all right to go home.'

The cabbie looked doubtful. 'You looks in a bloody awful state to me, mate. Still, if you've seen a doctor . . .' He looked in his mirror. 'They didn't do much to clean you up, did they?'

'I'm not wounded, just a bit shaken,' Linus said.

'The blood belongs to someone else, does it?' the cabbie commented. 'Which one was you in? Earl's Court or the MoD?'

'MoD?' Linus queried. Did that mean there had been a third explosion?

'Right by Earl's Court. Tall building. I 'ad a mate what worked there once. They organizes all their supplies from there, 'e said.'

So that's what the soldier meant, Linus thought. Aloud, he said, 'Both.'

The cabbie looked in his mirror again. 'Blimey! Glutton for punishment, in't yer?'

'Not exactly planned,' Linus told him and the man laughed.

'You ain't lost yer sense of 'umour, then. You *sure* you want Paddington?'

Actually, Linus was becoming less sure with every passing minute. The thought of a hospital bed and a ministering nurse became infinitely alluring. But so did home. Already Linus could feel himself crumbling at the edges. He thought he could hang on, keep himself together, for just as long as it took to close his own front door behind him. The doctor had said he was all right. He was beginning to feel distinctly not all right but the doctor should know best. Once he was home, he could sleep it off. That was all he needed. Lots and lots of sleep. He had lost all sense of chronology and was totally oblivious of the fact that the doctor's opinion had preceded the second explosion and might well be quite different if he saw Linus now. It would take an hour to get home. An hour and a half if he had to wait about for a train. He could hang on that long, maybe even a bit longer if he had to, but he hoped he wouldn't have to.

The taxi pulled into Paddington station. 'You sure about this, mate?' the driver said over his shoulder to Linus. 'I can still take you to an 'ospital. It won't be no trouble.'

'This'll be fine,' Linus assured him.

'Well, if you say so . . .' He still sounded uncertain. 'If you takes my advice, you'll clean yourself up a bit before you gets on a train.'

Linus thanked him but walked over to the destination board, not the cloakroom. He was scarcely aware that others on the concourse gave him a very wide berth or that a policeman watched him with more particular attention than he gave others. Linus found he had to read the board with a careful precision very different from the superficial scanning that was usually enough and even so, it was some minutes before his brain absorbed the information that no trains for Oxford were listed yet. He turned away then and studied instead the timetables posted towards the centre of the concourse. He found it very difficult to follow the timetable but he finally deduced that he had at least half an hour to wait. What had the taxi-driver said? He'd told him to clean himself up. He could do worse. It would help fill in the time and Linus wasn't sure he could last out half an hour without something to occupy him. He made his way to the men's cloakroom.

He didn't recognize himself at first. He looked in the

mirror and someone else looked out. A middle-aged man in what had once been a good suit, but the suit was dirty and crumpled, stained with something dark in some places while others had a light coating of coarse dust. Linus flicked it with his hand and the dust shifted around a bit but the dark stains remained where they were. The hand in the mirror was filthy with grime, like the hands of the winos that hung around Bonn Square and St Michael's-at-the-North Gate. The face, bearded and equally grimy, looked equally typical. It was an added shock to realize that this unkempt creature was himself. No wonder the taxi-driver had given him the advice he had. Linus ran water into the basin.

A paper towel does not become a sympathetic flannel and Linus winced as he tried to pretend it was, finally abandoning the attempt and using his fingers instead. His face was filthy. It hurt, too, and the pain was more than the pain of scrubbing off ingrained dirt. Some of the dirt, he discovered, was dried blood which seemed to have come from one cut on his forehead and another over the opposite eye. He took his time cleaning it off and needed to, because it was a painful process not made any easier by his dust-infested beard. His hands, too, looked better when he had scrubbed them, though he grimaced with distaste at the sight of his grimy, ragged fingernails. Finally, he took off his jacket and shook it out, an unexpectedly agonizing performance because his muscles were now beginning to stiffen up after the extreme, unwonted and unsought activity into which they had been plunged that day. He caught sight of the disapproving eye of the cloakroom attendant.

'Have you got a clothes-brush?' Linus asked him.

The man was at first undecided whether to deny any such possession but Linus's voice was at odds with his appearance. There was a slight West Country burr to it, but that notwithstanding, it was an educated voice, almost, the man thought, the voice of a gentleman.

'Yes, sir,' he said. 'If you'll wait a moment.'

He reappeared with the brush and took Linus's jacket from him, brushing it down with the brisk, professional touch of a batman. 'We seem to have been in the wars, sir,' he commented.

In many situations, Linus would have resented the use of the first person plural. From the cloakroom attendant it indicated a sympathetic solidarity which was welcome.

'There was a bomb at Earl's Court,' he said. 'It made a bit of a mess.'

The attendant was all contrition for the discourtesy he had nearly displayed. 'Were you in that, sir? I heard about it on the radio. Excuse me, sir, but don't you think you ought to go to a hospital? I can easily phone for an ambulance, if you like.'

Linus shook his head. 'Thanks, but no. I've seen a doctor. He said I could go.' He eased himself back into his jacket, grateful for the man's help, and fumbled in his pocket. 'I'm sorry,' he went on, 'I don't seem to have anything worthwhile by the way of a tip.'

The attendant was offended. 'That's not necessary, sir. Glad to do what I can. Will you be all right now?'

'What's the time?' Linus asked him and when the man told him he nodded. 'My train ought to be in by now. Yes, I'll be fine once I'm on board. Thanks for your help.'

Linus emerged on to to the concourse to find the homeward-bound rush had built up in the last quarter of an hour and it was quite painful threading his way to the destination board. Punctilious scrutiny finally produced the informationl he sought. His train was in and waiting on Platform Eight.

He had turned to make towards it when he caught sight of a familiar figure. His partially numbed mind could no longer deal with two issues at once, so it put the Oxford train to one side in order to concentrate on identifying the woman in question.

She seemed flustered, as if she had been delayed in the rush and had only just made it. She was small, elderly and grey-haired, and was looking anxiously at the destination-board as if afraid she had missed her train.

Suddenly the numbness cleared and Linus's brain began to function with the clarity and precision of a microscope under whose power the object being observed occupies the observer's full attention. Edith Ledwell! She had left Earl's Court . . . his mind wavered briefly. A long time ago. It seemed a lifetime but it could only be a few hours. Why was she still in London? Perhaps the delay was due to her having had to plant the Empress State bomb as well as the Earl's Court one. That would account for her having taken some time to get here. He remembered how the Ministry of Defence headquarters had collapsed. No. That was no opportunist bomb. The explosives that had wrecked that place had been planted with the care and precision with which a demolition expert brings down a chimney or a cooling-tower. Goodness only knew how or when those charges had been laid, but it hadn't been done by some little old lady with a brag-bag, and it probably hadn't been done that day. Someone with more expert knowledge than Linus Rintoul could work that one out and when they had, doubtless heads would roll, though probably no one outside Whitehall would ever learn whose.

Whatever had delayed her, here she was—and unaware of Linus's presence. He slipped back into the crowd a bit more. If she turned round, he would rather she didn't see him. He might look more like a tramp than Linus Rintoul, despite his efforts, but he wasn't prepared to bet on her not recognizing him. It began to look as if they would be travelling on the same train. He glanced up at the clock. There wouldn't be time to find a policeman and bring him back, let alone convince him of a highly improbable story. No. Get on the train too, and at least have the journey to decide what to do next. Should he get on ahead of her? If he did, and she saw him, at least she wouldn't assume he'd been following her. He rejected the idea. Better to make sure she was on the train before he joined it. He could make sure he picked a carriage some distance from hers, then she wouldn't even know he was on board.

He was nonplussed when, having scrutinized the overhead board, she turned in the opposite direction from the Oxford train and hurried under the gantry towards the left. Platform Two. A 125 Intercity train was waiting. Linus hastened along at what he judged to be a safe distance behind her. He glanced at the VDU at the barrier. Bristol. Bristol! He had a brief, law-abiding qualm. His ticket was for Oxford. Then he remembered it didn't matter. No one would look at it until he was on the train. They might make him get off at Reading or Didcot, and maybe his quarry would get off there as well. The worst they could do would be to charge him excess. No, his ticket was the least of his problems. He hurried after Edith Ledwell. Funny, he thought as he climbed aboard after she had already done so, he no longer thought of her as The Other One. The impostor had become for him, as for everyone else, the only one. And so she was, he reminded himself bitterly. The other one was dead.

Linus was no sooner aboard than the train began to move. It was packed and although Linus knew he looked a great deal more salubrious than he had done a short while before, he realized from the way in which people withdrew from him that he still looked a less than desirable travelling companion. There were no empty seats, he noted with dismay. He was getting to a stage when being able to sit down was likely to matter. He turned to a woman sitting on the gangway.

'Does this train go straight through to Bristol?' he asked.

She distanced herself infinitesimally from this disreputable-looking creature as if by so doing she could dissociate herself from the necessary answer. 'No. There are several stops.' Her tone was discouraging.

'Do you know which they are?' Linus couldn't afford to be deflected by an icy tone even if good manners told him he should.

Another passenger, a man, came to the woman's rescue. 'Reading and Swindon,' he said. 'Chippenham, I think, and possibly Slough. Oh, and Bath.'

Linus thanked him. He frowned. What was Edith Ledwell playing at? It was true she could change at Reading for Oxford or Banbury, but why do that if there was a train for Oxford leaving very shortly after this one? Reading and Swindon were both major junctions on the railway network. If he wasn't careful, she could get off at either and her eventual destination could be anywhere. He needed to have her in his sights so that if she did disembark, he would see her do so and could follow. Situated as he was at present, he couldn't even crane his neck to see if she got off. Unless she passed directly outside this carriage, he would have no way of knowing whether or not she was still on the train. He must get further forward and, ideally, in her carriage. He'd have to hope she was either facing forward or had managed to get a seat facing the engine. If not, she would certainly see him.

His unsavoury appearance gained him rapid progress through his own carriage and the next. He heard someone say, 'That sort shouldn't be allowed,' and guessed it referred to him. Further on, a woman leant confidentially across to her companion and said, 'He won't have a ticket. Still, he won't get away with it: they're very hot on that sort of thing on this service.' He paused in the little lobby at the end of the carriage and felt in his inside pocket. It would hardly be surprising after the events of the day if his ticket had gone. It was still there. It was a pity he had brought neither wallet nor cheque-book today. It had been a deliberate move designed to remove any temptation to spend money at Earl's Court. He had brought plenty of small change but most of that had gone on coffees, while his clip of pound coins had vanished, presumably having fallen out of his pocket during the day's vicissitudes. If they checked before Reading, he was all right. He could say he was changing there. After that, they'd just have to take his name and address. He pushed the ticket safely back in his pocket and glanced at the lights of a station as they speeded through. It didn't stop at Slough, then. He went into the next carriage.

As in the previous carriages, he stood just inside the door and peered cautiously first to one side of the standing passengers and then to the other. The high backs to the seats made it very difficult to identify anyone sitting with their back to him and it was usually impossible to check them until he was standing by each seat, looking down. The procedure was embarrassing at best and downright difficult when there were both sides of the central gangway to consider and that gangway was encumbered by those standing. His task was made a little easier by the fact that Edith Ledwell, too, had embarked only seconds before the train had drawn out. She was likely therefore either to be standing or to have a seat abutting the gangway. If she was standing, it wasn't in this carriage. Then he saw her. Edith Ledwell was at the far end of the carriage in a gangway seat—facing him.

Linus turned quickly away and his stomach lurched. He didn't think the recognition had been reciprocal. Not yet. If he stayed here it was inevitable that it would sooner or later become so. He stepped to the other side of the line of standing passengers, now blessing rather than cursing the obstruction they presented. Keeping his back to them, he edged his way down the carriage to the other end. It was no more difficult than it had been in the others: people simply did not want physical contact, however slight, with this refugee from a night shelter.

He stood in the lobby. There was room to breathe here and now that he knew where she was, he could relax until they came to a station. He peered out of the window. It was impossible to see far in the darkness outside but the lights from the train illuminated the thick snow beside the track. He had no idea where they were or how fast they were travelling because there was nothing outside by which he could gauge their speed. The smoothness of the ride, too, was deceptive.

They began to slow down for Reading well in advance of the station and Linus positioned himself so that he could see Edith Ledwell's sleeve and would know at once if she was proposing to get off here. The public address system announced Reading and Linus was taken aback when the voice added that they would stop there to pick up passengers only. No one could alight here. So she wasn't going to change here for Oxford or Banbury, he thought, and then found himself wondering how 'they' could stop someone alighting if they wanted to, once the train had stopped and the doors were opened. All the same, Mrs Ledwell was unlikely to want to draw that sort of attention to herself, no matter how safe she thought she was. Linus kept an eye on her, just in case, and was relieved that she made no attempt to leave her seat. Several people joined the train but few of them got on by the door through which they could see Linus. He noticed this and smiled wryly to himself. He obviously hadn't done as good a job in the cloakroom as he had thought.

As the train gathered speed once more, it occurred to him that he ought to have some sort of plan. Edith Ledwell might get off anywhere between here and Bristol and, of the stations yet to come, Swindon and Bristol itself were hardly small, one-platform affairs. She could disappear into the crowds. More probably, she could be met by a car or jump into a taxi, and Linus would be totally unable to follow her. It would be much easier if she could be taken on the train. The guard must be able to contact stations or signal-boxes along the route. Linus toyed with the idea of finding the guard and telling him his story. He rejected it. Even if the guard believed him enough to question Mrs Ledwell, she would—naturally—deny everything and Linus knew that if he were guard and faced with the choice of believing a sweet little old lady like Edith Ledwell or an unkempt, dirty, bearded tramp, the old lady would win every time.

No, he would tackle her himself. Of course she would be amazed, pretend never to have seen him before and very likely suggest the explanation for his charges lay either in drink or insanity, but it would create a fuss. The sort of fuss which would draw the guard and might even result in Linus's being thrown off the train—but for that he rather thought they needed the police and the police had a great fondness for witnesses, witnesses from whom they spent hours taking down statements. That would delay Edith Ledwell and give Linus time to convince them that his story was at least worth deeper investigation.

He pushed his way back down the carriage until he was level with her seat. There he turned.

'Why, Mrs Ledwell!' he exclaimed. 'It *is* Mrs Ledwell, isn't it?'

The first mention of her name just startled her but when she recognized the speaker, she noticeably paled. 'I think you've made a mistake,' she said, and Linus hadn't realized she could inject so much frozen acid into her voice.

'No mistake,' he said cheerfully. 'I came to see your dogs, remember? I remember you—very clearly. Saw you earlier today, actually, but couldn't chat. It was at Earl's Court. I was in the Kennel Club dining-room and saw you walk across the hall. Must have been getting on for three o'clock, I suppose.' He had the satisfaction of seeing her face go quite grey. He glanced down as if he were looking for something. 'Have you mislaid your brag-bag?' he asked. 'I did wonder when I saw you come back across the hall without it. Still, I don't suppose that bothers you in the circumstances, does it? I mean, you were lucky to get out when you did. You obviously weren't in the explosion.'

She was severely shaken, Linus noticed with grim satisfaction. She was not yet beyond recovery, however. 'You're drunk,' she said. 'Just look at you! I'm surprised they let you on the train! In the days when there was a ticket-collector at the barrier, they wouldn't have.'

Linus leaned over, resting one hand on the arm of her seat and put his face very close to hers. 'And do you know why, Mrs Ledwell? Because I *did* get caught up in the bomb. That's why I look like this. You know about the bomb, don't you? The one you had in your brag-bag. The one you left somewhere behind the Pedigree Petfoods stand—that bomb.'

She had pulled away from the bearded face so close to hers and Linus heard her say, 'You're mad,' but the words were a gesture for the bystanders, lacking any conviction.

Those same bystanders mistook the lack of conviction for an entirely understandable fear and came to her defence.

'Now look here,' one of them began. 'You can't talk to an old lady like that. Just you take yourself off or we'll send for the guard.'

'You do that,' Linus told him. 'Send for the guard, I mean. You do know a bomb went off at Earl's Court, I suppose? In the middle of Crufts dog show?' Their faces told him that at least some of them had heard. 'There was another one, too, almost immediately. It brought down the Ministry of Defence Headquarters. Now I don't know who planted the second one, but I'm reasonably sure she placed the first one. What's more, I told the police so. You fetch the guard, then he can ring ahead and the police can be waiting.'

'I don't know whether you're insane or just dead drunk,' one of the men said disgustedly, 'but of the two, I'd put my money on drunk. Look at him,' he went on to the carriage at large. 'Look at the way he's shaking. If that's not someone who's had three or four over the eight, I'm a Dutchman.'

'Please,' Edith Ledwell protested, 'there's no need for a fuss. Can't someone persuade him just to go away?'

'I'm not going away until they carry me off,' Linus told her. 'You know as well as I do that I'm not drunk.' He glanced away from her briefly and noticed that most of the standing passengers had melted away and the majority of those that had a seat were looking out of the windows at the fascination of the dark outside and thereby distancing themselves like true Brits from the unpleasant scene unfolding within the carriage.

'If that's the way you want it, I'm sure we can oblige,' the first bystander said. He looked around the carriage. 'Will someone fetch the guard?'

There was a long pause during which Linus began to fear that the national desire not to get involved might override the obvious common sense of getting someone like him removed. Then a young man who looked as if he might have been a student said, 'I'll fetch him. Which way is it?'

There were divided opinions on this but it was finally settled by the possible student going towards the engine while someone from the other end of the carriage reluctantly volunteered to seek the guard towards the rear of the train.

The guard was finally located and fetched and bore the appearance of a man bracing himself for an unpleasant task. One look at Linus convinced him that his apprehensions had been well founded.

'I gather you're being a bit of a nuisance, sir,' he said.

'No,' Linus replied. 'I'm being as much of a nuisance as I can. They just can't decide whether I'm barmy or drunk.'

'And which do you think it is?' the guard asked, thinking that he might achieve more by humouring the man.

'Well, I'm certainly not drunk,' Linus told him, 'and I was perfectly sane when I left home this morning. Of course, I hadn't been blown up then.'

'Ah yes. I gather you think you were in this Crufts bomb we've been hearing about. You weren't by any chance in the Brighton bombing as well, I suppose?'

'Don't be such a bloody fool,' Linus snapped in a voice so devoid of either alcohol or insanity and so full of authority that the guard was sufficiently taken aback to revise his original impression. 'Presumably you have the means of radioing ahead?' Linus went on.

The man nodded. 'We've got phones on these trains.'

'Then use them. Ring the police. Tell them it's Linus Rintoul. They'll probably need to check with the police in London. Tell them that, too—they'll not want to waste time unnecessarily.'

The guard looked at him doubtfully. 'I'll ring the Transport Police,' he said. 'We don't like people creating a disturbance on our trains even if they do think they've got a good reason.' He turned to the two men who had originally taken up the cudgels on Mrs Ledwell's behalf. 'Will you keep an eye on him till I get back?'

They replied that it would be a pleasure and he turned to Mrs Ledwell. 'Will you be all right for a few minutes, madam?' he asked.

'I suppose so,' she said doubtfully. 'It's just . . . well, I don't want to put everyone to all this trouble. I don't want to cause a fuss.'

'Now don't you worry about that,' the guard said kindly. 'We get his sort from time to time—though usually they're a lot younger and they've been to football matches,' he added, with a reproving glance at Linus. 'We'll soon have it all sorted out.'

He was gone some time and when he returned he seemed to be clearing the standing passengers out of the carriages and lobbies.

'Where are you putting everyone?' Linus asked.

'Made some room for them in First Class. It leaves the gangways clear for the time being,' the guard told him.

'D'you want this man in the guard's van?' one of Linus's minders asked.

The guard shook his head. 'We're carrying mail so we can't have every Tom, Dick and Harry who's had a few too many locked up with that little lot. No, he can stay here where we can all keep an eye on him. It won't be for long.'

It wasn't very long after that that Linus felt the train almost imperceptibly slowing down. 'Are we coming into Swindon?' he asked.

The guard glanced at his watch. 'No, not yet.'

The slackening speed became more noticeable. Maybe there was an incline or a bend, Linus thought.

Edith Ledwell got to her feet. 'Young man,' she said, addressing the guard who was, Linus thought, close to his own age. 'Would there be any objection if I . . .' She nodded in towards the carriage lavatory.

'Not so long as you finish before we stop, madam,' he said apologetically.

'Oh, I shan't be long,' she assured him.

Linus and the guard stood back to let her pass and Linus watched her. She appeared to be trying the door of the lavatory on the end of the carriage she had just left but it must have been engaged because almost at once she stepped over into the adjacent lobby, presumably to try that one before the train slowed down further. One could feel the brakes holding it back now.

'It must be Swindon,' someone said and Linus saw the guard look at his watch again.

'Is it?' he asked.

The guard shook his head.

They must be laying on an unscheduled stop, Linus thought, and glanced through the carriage towards the lobbies. No sign of Edith Ledwell. Suddenly he froze. Lavatories weren't the only things in the lobbies. 'The doors!' he shouted and pushed past the guard on his way to where he had last seen Mrs Ledwell. The guard was immediately behind him when the automatic doors between carriage and lobby slid back and they both clung to the aluminium frame as the cold air from outside hit them. The outer door on the left-hand side was wide open. There was no sign of Edith Ledwell.

'Oh my God! Pull the cord!' Linus said.

'No point,' the guard told him. 'We can't slow down any quicker. Maybe she's in the toilet.'

He thumped on the door but there was no answer. Linus reached across him and turned the handle. The door opened. The lavatory was empty. By the time they had checked that the other one was too, the train was nearly stationary.

Linus looked at the guard. 'Any chance . . .?' he asked.

The man shook his head. 'None at all. We can't have got down to much below forty when she went. She can't have survived that. An athlete couldn't have survived that.'

'What will have happened?'

'Not sure. Never had a case before, thank God, though it happens all the time. Usually they just run in front of the locomotive, though. She'll be back down the line a fair way. Two or three miles maybe. I'm not sure at that speed whether she'd have been sucked under. It'll have been quick, though. Mind you, it must have taken some strength to open the door at that sort of speed.'

'There was a lot about her that was deceptive,' Linus commented.

'Maybe there was, but she was still a little old lady,' the guard reminded him.

As far as Linus could tell, they had stopped at a place where the line ran over a stream and under a road. He could see no lights to suggest a village in the immediate locality but the lights of several vehicles on either side of the bridge indicated that the train driver had stopped exactly where he had been told to. Several policemen came forward and hauled themselves up into the carriage.

'What's all this about, then?' one of them said. 'Some sort of disturbance and talk of bombs? Sounds a bit far-fetched to me.'

Linus looked at him more sharply. The words were those of the traditional none-too-bright village bobby. They didn't fit the face or the manner. The man was nobody's fool but he had learned that it paid to be taken for one.

'It's a bit more than that now,' the guard said. 'A passenger fell out—or jumped—a bit further back. The old lady this man was pestering.'

Put like that, accurate though it undoubtedly was, it gave Linus a shock. It suggested she'd jumped because he had been 'pestering' her. Perhaps that was how it would strike other people. Linus had assumed she had risked killing herself in order to avoid being questioned by the police. What if his certainty about her villainy had been wrong? Where would that leave him? It wasn't a happy thought.

Word had already sped through the carriage that the old lady had jumped. No one could have accidentally opened a handleless Intercity door and fallen out. It would take a deliberate effort to lower the window and then lean out to open the door. No, she had jumped. The rumour was reinforced by the bobbing torch-lights now wending their way back along the track. Linus could feel the accusatory glares in his direction and supposed, philosophically, that he should be grateful no one had suggested she had been pushed. Yet.

'Now, sir,' the policeman began once he had taken down Linus's name and address. 'This old lady was known to you, I take it? Perhaps you can give me her name. Save us a lot of work later on.'

'Edith Ledwell,' Linus told him. 'At least—no, not really. She called herself Edith Ledwell. I don't know what her real name was.'

'I see.' He made no attempt to disguise his scepticism. 'She told you it wasn't her real name?'

'No, of course not. I knew the real Edith Ledwell. The one who was murdered in Norham Road. This woman was pretending to be her.'

The policeman flipped his notebook shut and replaced it in his pocket. 'I think, sir, the best thing will be for you to come along with us.'

He thinks I'm quite mad, Linus thought. Aloud, he said, 'Of course, Officer. There's just one thing, though. She wasn't alone. In the bombing, I mean. There's a young man who claims to be her son, though he's too young, really. Patrick. He's involved, too.'

'You saw him carrying bombs across Earl's Court, too, did you?'

'No, I haven't seen him at all today.'

'I see, sir. We'll bear it in mind. Now, if you'll just step down, you can sit in a nice, comfortable police car until we've verified that someone has fallen from the train and then we'll take you back to Swindon and get a statement from you. You'll be able to tell us all about it.'

Linus sighed. They were humouring him, presumably working on the principle that if they could keep him happy, he wouldn't suddenly become violent. He couldn't blame them but he was going to have a hard job convincing them and if Edith Ledwell was dead—as she almost certainly must be—any chance that she might confess to any part in recent events had vanished. He followed the policeman back to the lobby.

'Give Mr Rintoul a hand down,' the policeman called to colleagues on the track by the door and they obediently reached up to take his hands. It was a steep drop to the ground and the granite chippings were an uncomfortable landing-pad. Even with the policemen's help, Linus stumbled. He had expected to land on snow but the heat from passing trains had melted it this close to the track.

As he recovered from his stumble, he glanced up towards the front of the train which curved very slightly towards him, throwing a narrow circlet of light on to the snow, a reflection of the circlet of the windows. In that brief glance he saw the small rectangle of a window become the longer one of an open door and then a trousered silhouette jumped out, appeared to stumble in the darker area between the circlet and its reflection, before picking itself up and running across the reflection towards the strands of the fence that bordered the track.

It was a matter of seconds to take all this in and a few more for its significance to strike Linus.

'There's the other one!' he shouted, pulling away from the supporting hands and racing after the escaping figure. His sudden lunge towards the boundary fence took the policemen by surprise and by the time they had realized what was happening, Linus was through the wire and well on his way across the field in pursuit of his quarry which was clearly visible against the snow.

Running across that surface was easy for none of them and it lent the scene the slow-motion quality of a nightmare. Linus guessed that the fugitive had intended to slip away unseen and resume his journey next day which, since it had not occurred to Linus that Edith Ledwell's accomplice might also have been on the train, he could probably have done without rousing any suspicions. It didn't occur to Linus as he tried to develop a technique for getting through the snow at anything resembling speed, that the man he was chasing might not be Patrick Ledwell. Whether it was the circumstances or whether it was something about his shape as he jumped, Linus had no doubt at all about the identity of the man he was failing to gain on.

The police were shouting, as much at Linus as at the other man and Linus saw Patrick glance back over his shoulder. The sight of several pursuers seemed to make him hesitate briefly and Linus soon found out why when Patrick stopped altogether and turned, raising his hands in front of him. There was a flash of light followed by a sharp crack, and then another. Linus heard someone behind him cry out but he was too intent on closing the distance between himself and his quarry to look back. He ploughed on through the snow, regardless of the discomfort of wet shoes and soaking trouser-legs.

Patrick wasted no more time, either. He fired one more shot in the general direction of the pursuer who was closest, but did so without taking true aim and therefore missed. Then he changed direction and headed towards the stream.

Something in his movements had signalled his intention to Linus, who had already changed his own trajectory and was cutting across the wide arc, thereby closing still further the gap between them before Patrick's direction had perceptibly changed. The feeling that he was no longer attempting the impossible lent strength to Linus's legs and to his determination and he drew on such resources as his already war-torn body still harboured in order finally to close that gap.

Patrick's younger legs were tiring, too, but there was the black of a wood across the stream and if he could reach that haven, he stood a good chance of evading this immediate pursuit. But he reckoned without taking into account the way in which snow disguised irregularities and reached the stream at a place where the bank seemed level. As his feet sank almost up to the knee in a snow-filled hollow worn by generations of drinking cattle who chose here, and nowhere else, to water, Linus caught up with him and threw himself in a rugby tackle at the younger man's legs.

Together they went down and together they smashed into the icy stream. Linus's sole aim was to prevent the younger man from escaping. The shots that had been fired ensured that the police could not be far behind and that, whatever their views on Linus's sanity or sobriety might have been, they would not regard the man he had caught as an innocent passenger who grew tired of waiting.

The police might not have been far behind but it seemed to take them an age to catch up. Linus felt his hands growing numb with the effort of hanging on to Patrick in the bitter water and it was with no reluctance at all that he finally relinquished his captive into the more efficient custody of the professionals.

'It is him,' Linus said. 'Mrs Ledwell's son. He's a telephone engineer,' and with that non sequitur he passed out.

The hospital kept Linus in overnight and then sent him home by ambulance. They told him all he needed was rest and sleep, and they got in touch with Sean to make sure he was on hand to see to it that Linus did as he was told. Linus's own doctor visited later in the morning and examined him thoroughly. It was a painful procedure because, although by some miracle Linus had broken nothing, he was black and blue—not to mention a few colours in between—with bruises. Dr Wilcote was less than sympathetic.

'Making up for our lost youth, are we?' he asked sarcastically.

'It must look like that,' Linus agreed.

When the doctor had taken his leave after confirming the hospital's prescription of rest and sleep, Inspector Lacock's arrival prevented Linus's putting the prescription into operation.

'D'you feel up to talking?' he asked.

'Talking? Or making a statement?'

'The statement can come later. That will deal with the facts. I want to know what was going on in your mind.'

Linus looked at him warily. 'Which diagnosis do you favour—insanity or intemperance?' he asked.

'Neither, as a matter of fact, though I could build a case for both. Just tell me the story from the beginning.'

'It gets complicated,' Linus warned.

'Then I'll make myself comfortable,' the Inspector said and brought a chair round to the bedside. 'Your son's bringing us up some coffee. I'm in no hurry.'

Linus told him the mixture of events and deductions from the time he met the real Edith Ledwell in the Randolph. He had no difficulty remembering what had happened or the conclusions he had drawn but he found it wasn't always easy to get them in the correct sequence, because hindsight had given him connections that had not been apparent at the time. Inspector Lacock rarely interrupted him and then only for clarification of a particular point. When Linus had finished, he said, 'Why didn't you come to us with these suspicions?'

Linus shrugged. 'I thought about it—several times. You've got to admit, it was a pretty far-fetched theory. I could see myself being laughed out of St Aldate's Police Station.'

'That doesn't mean the story wouldn't have been checked out.'

'Maybe. It's academic now. Tell me, how much of it fits the facts you know?'

The Inspector hesitated. 'Terrorism's not my field and

there are bodies involved that aren't accountable to the police. It's early days, too, of course. I believe they've managed to identify the woman who posed as Edith Ledwell. The Garda say she's got no record in the Republic and the Ulster police don't have anything on her, either, but a deeper check reveals that both her parents were very active in the Troubles—her father was hanged for taking effective pot-shots at British troops. She's supposed to have emigrated to the States but now we know better—it was about that time that she slipped in here and established herself as the returned Edith Ledwell. It seemed she learned the lessons of her upbringing all too well. The current theory is that she was indeed a "sleeper", planted to establish herself in the dog fancy all those years ago with this very plan in mind: to create a diversion to blow up Crufts and then, under cover of the chaos that would cause, to hit the real target, the place from which the Ministry of Defence organizes, among other things, all the supplies needed for all the armed services—the Empress State Building.'

'Not Whitehall?'

'Apparently not.'

'I thought it was a block of flats.'

'I gather it's purpose isn't much advertised.'

Linus frowned. 'So they settled on Crufts as a suitable diversionary vehicle, but how on earth did they settle on Mrs Ledwell?'

Inspector Lacock shrugged. 'Our lot are working on that. At the moment the theory is that, having settled on the cover story—and presumably having some choice of "sleepers" available—they dug back through the canine press till they found someone who fitted the bill: well-known enough for the papers to report their emigration and physically close enough to fit an available sleeper. After that, it's just a matter of careful organization and a lot of money.'

Linus still looked doubtful. 'There's a flaw in that

argument somewhere. She's been in those Truffle Dogs for a long time. I don't think Crufts was held at Earl's Court in those days.'

'It wasn't. It used to be Olympia—still near enough to make a diversion effective. The move to Earl's Court a few years ago was a bonus and now that there are mutterings that even Earl's Court isn't big enough and the suspicion that the Kennel Club may be looking elsewhere, they decided to strike. The NEC wouldn't suit their purpose at all.'

'So she did plant that bomb?'

'They think so. It was put in the car the Guide Dogs people used in their demonstration. A nice sheet of flame as the petrol tank exploded on the only vehicle in the building. An incendiary device, of course. Napalm, I gather. Jellied petrol, to you. Packed about with bits of metal for maximum effect. Very nasty.'

'What about the son?'

'Almost certainly no relation, though they can't be sure just yet. Not as young as he looks and definitely on record. They know who he is, all right. Hadn't been seen or heard of for years. Now we know why. Whoever was responsible for losing track of him in the first place will wish they hadn't, but that's not our business. He's the real expert. God knows how he got close enough for long enough to plant all those charges—there's going to be a few resignations over that little slip-up, I shouldn't wonder, but he certainly did a highly professional job. It seems to have been sheer chance they were on the same train, though the feeling is he saw her get on but she was probably unaware that he was on board, too. They don't know what held her up, but she was almost certainly meant to be on an earlier train.'

'Destination?'

'Bristol. We put two and two together just too late to stop the ship from leaving. If it goes into Irish waters, they'll board it. Won't find anything, though. After all, we've got the cargo.'

Linus was thoughtful. 'If I'd come to you with my theory, maybe all this could have been stopped,' he suggested.

'Maybe. More likely the only thing to have been abandoned would have been the Crufts bomb. There's plenty of other opportunities to get into Earl's Court.' Inspector Lacock stood up. 'You look tired. Someone will come and take a formal statement from you, but it can wait.' He hesitated. 'I'm afraid you're going to find you've got a bodyguard for a while. At least until after you've given evidence. Can you live with that?'

'It sounds as if I might not live without it,' Linus said.

The Inspector laughed. 'An incautious use of words.' He reached the door and then turned to look at Linus. 'You know, Rintoul, you must lead the least boring life of any civil servant in the country.'

'I'll trade it in any time,' Linus assured him.